CONSORT OF LIGHT

THE WITCH'S CONSORTS #5

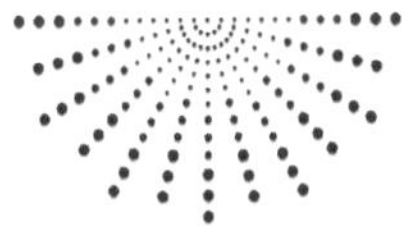

EVA CHASE

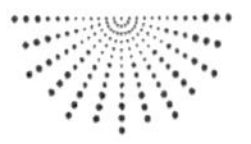

CHAPTER ONE

Rose

$\mathcal{I}$ hadn't expected that I'd be making my next trip to the Witching Assembly building with all my unsparked consorts at my side. I *definitely* hadn't expected we'd be making the trip in a chauffeured limo. But here I was, tucked into the back seat between Gabriel and Damon with Seth, Kyler, and Jin across from us, noticing every bump of the wheels as the sleek vehicle raced along our country roads toward Portland.

We understand there have been many recent attempts to harm both you and your consorts, Gwen Remington, the high-ranking Assembly official who'd called for my presence, had said on the phone. *It's in everyone's best interests to ensure you arrive here safely.* And witching society wasn't very good at doing things by half measures. So, a limo it was.

I guessed Remington saw me as some kind of

valuable property now. My consorts and I were among the few who'd known about the demons lurking at the edge of our world, other than the witching families who'd secretly summoned those demons and gained strange powers from them. I couldn't blame her if she didn't want to trust the criminals. If the demons had really broken through the portal on that cliffside just a few hours from Portland, like Remington had said, then all witching kind and unsparked too might be screwed if we couldn't come up with a solution fast.

"What exactly did the Assembly say has happened out at the Cliff?" Ky asked, leaning forward with an intent expression on his freckled face. He had his phone out in his slim hand, poised as if to take notes from my answer—which maybe he *was* planning on doing. My computer-aficionado consort never met a topic he wasn't ready to research. "How did the demons get through the portal *now?* What are they doing?"

"Not much, so far," I said. "And it sounds like there's only the one demon actually out. Remington said they suspected its escape had something to do with that guard of Frankford's who fell over the Cliff... That maybe her death gave a boost to their powers."

My voice dropped for the last bit. The guard had fallen because she'd been pushed—by the witch who was coming to the Assembly with us, Thalia Ainsworth, sitting in the front seat next to the driver right now.

Thalia probably couldn't hear me through the privacy screen anyway, but I didn't want to make her feel guilty. She'd been through enough already. The faction that had been negotiating with the demons had gotten their hooks into who-knew-how-many witches whom they'd forced to use magic to keep the creatures in line. Thalia had been having her spark drained like that for years, maybe decades. It'd been hard enough for her to go anywhere near the Cliff. She'd only shoved the guard out of the way with a spell because the other woman had been about to attack Remington.

"Is that a common thing?" Jin asked, tipping his head to the side. "Death affecting magic like that?" He'd been more involved in the actual magical side of my life than any of my other consorts in the last few weeks, using his artistic skills to paint glyphs I could imbue with protection spells. His lithe fingers were still stained with different colors that hadn't quite washed off after his last painting session.

"That kind of release of energy—it's bound to have an effect," I said. "It's not something we usually explore very much in witching society, though. Harming animals, let alone people, for the magical gain is against Assembly law. The closest I've ever gotten is burning plant materials."

"But it's not as if a bunch of demons are going to take the high road," Damon muttered, tucking his arm around mine. His dark blue eyes flashed. "If the thing I saw in that cave even has a concept of morality."

"Probably not," I said. "But *we* still have to be careful how we handle it. We don't know how the demon's going to respond to... well, anything we do."

Damon grimaced, but he didn't argue. He did have a habit of jumping into a fight full-throttle without thinking things through a whole lot in advance.

Something we'd chided him for plenty of times in the past. But sometimes that passion did work out in our favor.

"Anyway," I went on, "the one that escaped hasn't caused much trouble yet, from what Remington said. It's kind of meandering across the area just east of the coast, pretty slowly, like it's getting its bearings. It's knocked over a few fences and burned some patches of grass, but thankfully there aren't a whole lot of people in that part of the county. The Frankfords chose an isolated spot for their secret dealings. We just can't assume the demon is going to stay that passive."

"And we don't know that more of them won't push through too," Ky said.

"Exactly." I worried at my lower lip. "The bindings on the portal itself might be weaker than they used to be. My dad made it sound as if they *needed* me to make sure they could keep the demons contained."

"Hey." Gabriel squeezed my knee reassuringly, shifting his weight to offer even more of the warmth of his body. "This isn't your fault in any way, Rose. The Frankfords and the people with them were turning those witches into *slaves*. None of those women deserved that. You definitely didn't."

"I know," I said quietly. As much as the thought of my father brought a flare of anger into my chest now, sometimes it was still hard to believe that the man who'd raised me, mostly alone, could have been planning that kind of fate for me—even though he'd admitted as much to my face when we'd finally discovered what the Frankfords' faction was hiding on the Cliff.

But Gabriel sounded so confident, like he always did, that the pinch of guilt over my potential responsibility faded. That faction couldn't have gone on like it was. We'd had to find a way to stop it. The problem had just gotten a lot more complicated.

Seth frowned where he was sitting next to his twin. The two of them would have been identical if Seth hadn't kept his tawny hair cropped shorter than Ky's wild curls and his body bulked up with regular work-outs and the labor he did for his dad's renovation business.

"How is the Assembly going to feel about the five of us being there with you?" he asked. "I know they weren't all aware of the Frankfords' vendetta against us, but they've still been punishing—maybe even *murdering*—witches who got into relationships with guys from outside your community, haven't they?"

"I don't know how many people in the Assembly knew about that part either," I said. "Ky, you found those records in some super-secret section of their network, didn't you?"

Kyler nodded. "It was blocked off inside an already secure part of the Justice Division's files. Definitely not full-access to all the employees."

"So it's not an open policy. But we will have to be careful." I twined my fingers with Damon's and squeezed. "That's part of the reason I insisted that they accept you all coming with me. If anyone was going to try to hurt you, it'd be a lot easier for them to do it when I'm hundreds of miles away. And pretty much everyone in the Assembly is going to see our consorting as strange. After all, everyone working with the Frankfords has been destroying evidence of these kinds of relationships in the past, attacking anyone who crosses that line... I don't even know how far back that goes. Maybe even before they started dealing with the demons."

Why? Just to take as much power and choice from witching women as they could? Did they envy our magic that much? My stomach twisted at the thought.

"They need us right now anyway," I added. "They've got a much bigger problem, and no one else who can help the same way. And they can't exactly sweep our relationship under the rug—it's pretty out in the open now."

"Some of them will come around," Jin said. "Your one aunt and your cousin—that whole branch of the family—they were totally welcoming."

"Yeah." I wished I had them here right now too. But my aunt Ginny was on the other side of the country, and Remington had immediately vetoed the idea that any of the other witches staying on my estate come with us. *For now, we'd like to limit exposure to those already well-exposed,* she'd said. My cousin Naomi had stayed behind with one of the witches who'd come to me for help after her family, aligned with the Frankfords' faction, had tried to force a corrupted consorting.

"Whatever happens, we'll be there with you the whole way," Gabriel said.

Damon shot him a dark look. "Says the guy who *hasn't* been here most of the last two weeks?"

"Hey!" I said before Gabriel had to defend himself. "We know why Gabriel left. He was looking out for us even if he wasn't nearby, even if we didn't know it at the time. I get that you didn't like it, but *we* have bigger problems now too. We have to stand by each other—be a united front."

"I'm ready to take them on: Assembly, demons, whatever," Ky said with a grin and a mock salute.

Damon let out a ragged breath, but he slumped back in the seat at the same time. "I am too," he said in a resigned voice.

Gabriel ducked his head close to mine and brushed his lips over my cheek. My pulse skipped a beat at the tender gesture. It had been a rough time without him—thinking he'd left because I'd horrified him in my attempts to push back against the Frankfords and their allies. But maybe I'd needed that pain to remind me of the witch I wanted to be.

My newest consort had only just come back to us today. I believed him that he wouldn't leave again, but it might take a little while before my heart completely recovered.

My head felt too muggy to process much more information or emotion right now. It'd been a long day, and we'd already made the trip between my estate and the Cliff twice. Earlier today I'd had to fight for my life and the lives of my consorts. I'd been looking forward to curling up in bed for a nice long sleep.

Instead, I snuggled closer to Gabriel, setting my head on his shoulder. "I think we should all get as much rest as we can. We're going to want to go into this situation clear-headed."

"I can't argue with that," Seth said, propping his arm against the window as a sort of pillow. Ky yawned and stretched his legs out as well as he could in the space between us, his foot coming to rest against mine. I let my eyes drift closed.

Impeding demon battles and all, I was so worn out it couldn't have been more than a few minutes before I was out like a light.

The jerk of the limo coming to a stop woke me up. My head had slid down to Gabriel's chest—he had his arm around my back, his own head tipped next to mine until the second he snapped awake too. Damon shoved himself upright, his fingers still twined in my grasp. The guys across from us rubbed bleary eyes and yawned. I didn't think any of us had gotten close to a decent night's rest.

The privacy screen rolled down. "The Assembly building," the driver said. "They're waiting for you."

It was still night outside, the dark sky hazed with the city's lights and the downtown street outside the Assembly building quiet. Only one other car rumbled past as we made our way to the broad glass door in the modern gray structure. A damp pressure weighed on the air, as if a storm might be brewing. Hopefully only out here and not in there.

A couple of witches in the trim sweats the Assembly enforcers liked to wear had come to the entrance to meet us. One woman's eyes widened as she took in my consorts, and the other's lips curled in what looked like disdain. My jaw tightened, but I managed not to bristle.

"I understand you have a spell binding you that you need taken off?" the first woman said to Thalia.

Thalia opened her mouth and hesitated. The

binding prevented her from even acknowledging there was a binding.

"She does," I said quickly, and the older witch shot me a grateful glance.

The first enforcer motioned for Thalia to follow her, and they disappeared down the hall. The second beckoned us with a flick of her hand.

I'd been in the Assembly building before—to discuss a couple of projects I'd worked on that involved their archives, to apply for my original consorting—but the pale gray halls had never felt quite this imposing then. Maybe it was the darkness beyond the windows, or the drone of the air conditioning system... or maybe it was just the reason I was here, hanging over us.

The enforcer came to a stop at a door around a bend in the hall and eased it open. "Lady Hallowell and her consorts," she said in introduction, and I was almost completely sure I caught a hint of a sneer at the last word. But there wasn't time to worry about that, because with a couple more steps, we were faced with some of the most powerful figures in my witching society's government.

My gaze shot first to the officials I'd seen most recently. Gwen Remington, the head of the International Affairs Division, stood near the head of the long narrow meeting table, her frosted silver-blond hair pulled back in a gold clip and her broad shoulders tensed even as she gave us a small smile as a welcome. Next to her, Justin Brimsey, the head of Unsparked Relations, ran a hand over his gray-and-chestnut buzz-cut, his expression wary. Miriam Travers, a petite witch with an auburn bob from the Finances division who'd accompanied the two higher officials out to the Frankfords' property yesterday, stood farther down the table. They were the only members of the Assembly who'd witnessed the demons and their portal directly.

The other officials I recognized either vaguely or not at all, other than the couple at the head of the table, who'd turned as we arrived. Eleanor and Joseph Northcott had presided over the entire Assembly for the past eight years. They made a matching set, both of them tall and lean, her braided hair an only slightly lighter shade of gray than his slicked-back waves. Eleanor's mouth pursed as she took us in; Joseph looked as if he'd just barely managed to catch his eyebrows before they rose. I guessed that reaction was better than horror.

I got to be relieved for the approximately two seconds before one of the less familiar officials down the table, a stern woman with angular features, said, "What are *they* doing here?"

My back had already stiffened before Remington confirmed who the other woman had been referring to.

"Lady Hallowell requested the presence of her consorts," she said. "It appears they have been as involved in this matter as she has been, so they may have additional insights."

"They're unsparked," the other witch protested. "We can't—"

Lady Northcott raised her hand. "The decision has already been made."

"Not by us," a younger man across the table said. "I

don't think having unsparked individuals privy to our internal discussions is a wise idea either. If we allow—"

The guys were stirring uneasily behind me. My hands balled at my sides. "If you *don't* allow them to stay, then I leave too," I said. "Is that a clear enough decision for you? My consorts know *more* than I do about the demons in some ways. Are we going to stop this monster, or did you want to spend your time playing out old prejudices?"

The man shut up. Mr. Northcott gave us a grim smile. "The demon is our first priority, of course. I apologize. We don't know how quickly we might need to act. Are you ready to get down to business right away?"

I would have loved another few hours' sleep, preferably on an actual bed, and I'd bet my consorts wouldn't have minded that either. But the thought of the horrific creature I'd been faced with in the Frankfords' cave was more than enough to keep me alert.

"We'll do what we can," I said. "Let's get started."

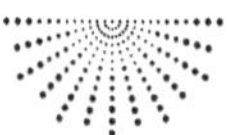

CHAPTER TWO

Jin

"None of the elemental spells our enforcers attempted have resulted in any noticeable effect on the demon's behavior either," said the older guy who seemed to jointly rule over this room—Mr. Northcott, one of the other officials had called him. He and his wife had been doing most of the talking during this meeting. The other people they'd pulled together seemed to mostly be there to nod and murmur agreement whenever those two weren't completely sure of their assessment.

"None at all?" Rose asked. She'd been given a seat at the table—and the other officials had rearranged themselves to offer us seats around her. I wasn't sure how much that'd been in deference to her and how much because they didn't really want to be mixed in with us intruders.

Lady Northcott shook her head, her light gray braid swaying against her back. "No change in the direction it was moving, no change in its speed, no sudden reactions. The enforcers might as well not have been magicking at it at all."

The woman who'd earlier tried to argue that none of us consorts should be in the room piped up, her gaze carefully avoiding me and the other guys. "The squads out there have attempted to record video of their attempts for the rest of us to try to analyze, but something about the demon's presence seems to affect the equipment badly. The images are too blurred to be useful."

Rose nodded, and I remembered the garble that was all Gabriel had managed to get on his phone's recording. Too bad, or we might have avoided ending up at this point altogether.

"What about glyphs?" my consort said. She glanced at Kyler beside me. "Didn't the files say something about a few different glyphs the Frankfords and the others had been using?"

"I think there were three," Ky said. He'd spent more time pouring over those files than the rest of us combined. "It sounded like at least one of them was used to strengthen the barrier around the portal. I didn't pay a lot of attention to that part since it wasn't going to help us expose what was going on, but if I can get access to the files here, I should be able to find the reference quickly enough."

The skeptical woman exchanged a glance with the man who'd also been hesitant about us being here. They had no idea how much a bunch of unsparked people really could contribute, did they? I fished my protective pendant out from beneath my shirt and displayed it for the officials to see, offering a faint grin at the same time.

"I've been pretty impressed by what your glyphs can offer. I made these for all of us as protection, and it only took Rose a few minutes to magic them up." I traced my finger over the glyph hidden in the miniature painting. "We completely fended off an attack from a bunch of enforcers who were working for the Frankfords' faction thanks to work like this inside our vehicle."

"Those defended you against witching magic," the hesitant guy said. "A demon is something completely different, as we're already seeing."

I held up my hands. "Oh, I know, and I know that it's a lot more Rose's magic than my painting skills that do the trick anyway. But... we got pretty far just by making use of every strategy we could, when we were up against a much more powerful force. So maybe the same approach will work here." I shrugged, still smiling. I wasn't going to tell these people what to do, but they should know we were willing to pitch in.

The gazes on us five guys felt a little less hostile and a little more curious now, at least.

"We can certainly try to make use of the glyphs mentioned once we've read over the notes regarding them," Lady Northcott said, with a slight bob of her head. "Given the speed with which this situation has developed, we haven't had time to fully assess the records you passed on. This is exactly why we needed you." She turned to Kyler, motioning to one of the officials near the end of the table at the same time. "Can I get you started pulling up the relevant documents right away?"

Ky's narrow jaw gave a nervous twitch, but he nodded. "Sure. Just show me where I can get to work."

"He should be given as much respect as any member of witching society," Rose said warily as the lesser official came around to escort Ky out of the room.

"Of course," Mr. Northcott said. "We'll set up a full office for your use here, as long as you need it."

Rose squeezed Ky's hand before he left, her gaze trailing after him for a moment before she turned back to the table. Damon jumped in before anyone else could speak.

"You're all talking as if we've got to start from scratch here. The Frankfords and the rest of those assholes were controlling these demons, keeping them in that cave, for decades, weren't they? With the witches they were roping in to do their dirty work? They should know how to push this thing back."

Lady Northcott rubbed her mouth. "We've started reaching out to the witches from the families mentioned in the records to try to determine who has been involved and to what extent. Before we'd heard of the demon's escape, we'd already called a few of the witches closer by to meet with us here so that we could remove the spells preventing them from speaking up and to take their accounts. But the experience seems to have... affected them badly. I'm not sure they'll be ready to take up any sort of fight as quickly as we may need them."

Rose frowned. I'd bet she was thinking about that older witch, Thalia, who'd joined us on the estate and come with us here. I remembered how worn down the woman had looked when I'd first seen her, drifting along as if she were more a ghost than a living person.

"They've been through so much already," she said. "It doesn't seem fair to ask even more of them."

I set my hand on her arm. "You could always just talk to them. There doesn't need to be any pressure involved."

"They know what those demons are like better than anyone," Gabriel said. "Most of them must want to help, even if they don't want to be on the front lines."

"You have seemed to present yourself as a safe presence to those in need of one, Lady Hallowell," Gwen Remington said, her silver-blond hair glinting as she dipped her head. "It might not be a bad thing for you to talk with them and simply see what they're able to contribute at this point, once it's morning."

I could see the hesitation still in Rose's stance. My consort had tried so hard to protect the few witches who'd come to her for help and felt so horrible when she couldn't completely. Did she think she might somehow hurt these poor women more than the demon would if it unleashed its full powers on the world?

Maybe she just needed the reminder that she wasn't in this alone—not in any way.

"I'll come with you," I said. "I can make them all their own pendants, whatever glyph they'd like incorporated. It might not protect them from everything out there, but it's a start, right?"

Rose relaxed a little and shot me a smile. "That sounds like a perfect idea."

* * *

I might have been in a building owned by a secret society I hadn't even known existed a few months ago, surrounded mostly by people who saw me as something less than them, but there was something about the tangy scent of paint that always made me feel at home. One of the officials had found a flip chart display stand I could use as a makeshift easel, and Rose had somehow convinced another to do a quick run to a local art store. Now I was setting up my materials in the brightest corner of the lounge room where we were meeting with the formerly demon-enslaved women the Assembly had collected.

Mid-morning light was streaming through the room's two windows now, traffic sounds from the busy street outside carrying faintly through the glass. The four women the Northcotts had ushered in had stopped in a cluster by one of the sofas. They ranged in age from a wan young woman who looked younger than Rose to an elderly lady whose hair was a pure ivory-white that my fingers itched to commit to canvas. But all of them looked drained, even though they'd just gotten up for the day.

"You're going to paint us... necklaces?" the youngest witch, who'd been introduced as Crystal, asked in a thin voice.

"Pendants, like mine," I said, showing off my own like I had in the meeting earlier. "They've gotten us through a lot of messes."

"It's like wearing a bit of magical armor," Rose said, tugging out her own so they could see it. "Jin's gotten a lot of practice incorporating the glyphs into his art. We could do a standard protective one, or if there's one you feel would make you even more secure against the demon's influence...?"

"I'd like one like yours," Crystal said. "Blue and purple, if you can customize the colors."

"Of course." I twirled my paintbrush. "I might not be magical, but I've got to think the spell will work better if the painting itself speaks to you too."

"That makes a certain kind of sense," the elderly woman—Selena—said. Her voice was paper dry.

"Have the Assembly officials told you much about the current situation?" Rose asked tentatively as I got to work. All four of the witches had expressed relief at being rescued and contentment with how the Assembly had handled their cases so far, but it also didn't take magic to tell their experiences had taken a huge toll on them.

"One of the demons got loose from the Cliff," Crystal said with a shudder, hugging herself.

"Bloody Frankfords," Selena muttered. "Messing with forces they couldn't possibly fully comprehend, let alone control." Her hand shook as she smoothed it over her pinned-back hair.

"We're hoping you won't ever have to be anywhere near the Cliff or the demons again," Rose said. "But we figured some extra magic to ward off ill-intent couldn't be a bad thing."

A murmur of agreement passed through the witches. I paused as I finished the last curve of the glyph. The acrylic paint needed to dry before I could incorporate the rest of the design.

"There were some glyphs mentioned in the Frankfords' files," I said in as light a tone as I could manage. "If any of those helped hold the demons on the other side of their portal, I should probably be painting *that* all over this building."

A halting giggle escaped Crystal. "That would be an interesting look."

Eloise, a middle-aged witch whose hands were nearly as weathered as Selena's, shook her head. "We never used the glyphs they'd constructed for that purpose," she said hollowly. "Those symbols... They were meant to transfer power. From us to..." Her mouth twisted.

"It's okay," Rose said gently, touching her elbow. "You don't have to talk about it."

"We should, though," Selena said, squaring her shoulders. "We don't have time for weakness, not if one of those fiends is rambling around. They stole our magic, and then the men claimed some of the demons' power for themselves. That's what she's talking about." The words came out firmly, but her chin wobbled at the end of her declaration.

"So you and they didn't use *any* glyphs as part of securing the portal?" I checked.

"Not that I remember," Crystal said, and the other witches shook their heads in turn.

"Well, that's too bad," I said, still lightly but softer now. "Here I was hoping to add demon-banisher to my resume."

Crystal giggled again. She looked down at her hands.

"The magic they had us do to hold the portals in place... It wasn't like anything I ever got taught. No one does spells like that these days."

"Barbaric," Eloise bit out.

When they didn't continue, I went back to dabbing color on the wooden token that would become Crystal's pendant. Rose waited too, giving them space to decide what and how much to say.

"We don't have a binding stopping us from talking now," Eloise added finally. "But even so, it's not easy."

"That's fine," I said. "We're here to offer something to you, not to take."

Something about those words seemed to unlock Crystal's limbs. She shoved the filmy sleeve of her blouse up her arm in a jerky motion. A raw red line, only recently scabbed, stood out against her pale skin.

"Blood," she said. "Skin and hair and nails too, sometimes, but mostly blood. That's how they had us seal the demons in."

CHAPTER THREE

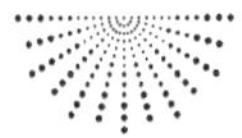

Rose

"How close will we be able to get to the demon without provoking it?" I asked.

Investigator Ruiz glanced back from where she was sitting in the front passenger seat of the jeep. The breeze from the partly open window ruffled her black pixie cut. "The enforcers who've been in the field monitoring the demon have managed to stay within about a hundred feet. I wouldn't recommend getting any closer unless you think you're ready to take it on."

Beside me in the back, Justin Brimsey made a faint snorting sound. The head of Unsparked Relations had opted to come with me on this scouting mission, and I was getting the impression it was because he didn't entirely trust me to handle myself properly out there. As if it were so bizarre to say I'd like to get a look at the thing we were trying to stop before making definite plans to tackle it.

At least I was pretty sure Ruiz was on my side. We'd first met when she was inquiring about the witches who'd suddenly left their homes to take shelter on my estate, and I hadn't always been capable of being up front with her. But when I'd needed back-up on the Frankfords' property by the Cliff, she'd come. She was the one who'd arrested Charles Frankford.

Pebbles rattled against the jeep's undercarriage. The driver wasn't pushing our speed on the country lanes near the coast where the demon was still lurking, but the roads weren't the best maintained I'd ever driven on. The breeze was warm and slightly damp, even though the sun was shining overhead. It carried a bit of ocean salt.

"You said you wanted to observe the thing, Lady Hallowell," Brimsey said. "I hope you intend to restrict yourself to that. You can hardly be prepared to engage."

"I'm not planning on trying to 'engage'," I said, suppressing a prickle of irritation. "I know my limitations."

He made another of those derisive sounds. "Oh, do you?" he muttered.

I shifted in my seat to face him. We had farther to go before we'd be in sight of the demon. Maybe it'd be better to tackle *this* problem before it went any farther, and without my consorts here to have to listen to whatever garbage he was going to say about them.

"If you have an issue with me, why don't we hash that out now, Mr. Brimsey?" I said. "The Assembly called me here asking for my help. I'm not sure what I could have done wrong before now in your eyes. I did everything I could to expose the Frankfords' crimes to the Assembly as soon as I knew about them. I didn't take any risks without feeling they were my only real option—you can be sure of that."

Brimsey eyed me warily for a moment, his lips pursing. He had a burly frame, but it wasn't all muscle by any means. Jowls were starting to form on either side of his rounded jaw.

"It's not clear to me that your decisions in regards to your consorting stayed within the realm of necessity," he said.

I would have liked for him to have said something different, but I couldn't pretend I was surprised. "You lead the Unsparked Relations Division," I pointed out. "Out of anyone, shouldn't you have a little respect for the unsparked?"

He grimaced. "I maintain the divide between witching society and theirs—and *that* is out of necessity. Do you have any idea the complications that arise when they come across proof of our activities?"

"My consorts haven't caused any complications."

"Yet."

"And it didn't use to be unheard of for witches and unsparked men to mix," I said. "There's been a campaign, probably involving the Frankfords but going back at least a few generations, to destroy all evidence of those relationships. But the history is there. I'm not the only one who's seen scraps they missed."

"That may be the case," Brimsey said. "I doubt there have been many witches at any time who took not just one unsparked consort but five, though. What necessity prompted that?"

I opened my mouth, paused, and closed it again. What could I possibly say that would make him understand? Maybe nothing.

I gave it a try anyway. "Are you consorted, Mr. Brimsey?"

His eyes narrowed. "I am. To one woman, who has no other consorts."

"Do you love your wife?"

He stared at me for a moment before sputtering, "What does that have to do with anything?"

"Just answer the question," I said. "Hopefully it's not too difficult."

"Of course it's not. I wouldn't be consorted to her if there were no love between us."

"All right. Can you explain exactly why you feel that way about her? The feelings that made you want to tie your life to hers?"

His jaw worked. He looked away from me, scowling. "We're well-suited for each other. I'm not going to get into private details."

"I'm not asking you to," I said. "But you couldn't really explain the feelings even if you wanted to, could you? There's something at a gut level that you can't simply lay out with logic."

"Where are you going with this?"

My mouth twisted into a crooked smile. "That's why I can't justify to you why I have five consorts, Mr. Brimsey. It felt right. It would have felt wrong to not be with all of them. I could give you a long story about childhood bonding and trust and finding strength in each other, but in the end it'd still come down to that. I love all of my consorts. We all know it's best when the six of us are together. I don't really see how our decision is any business of yours when it hasn't hurt you or the Assembly."

"It'll draw attention from your unsparked neighbors."

"Oh, I'm sure it already has. But, you know, that kind of distracts them from thinking about what witchy things might be happening on the estate. There were plenty of rumors about the mysterious Hallowell family before I ever laid eyes on any of the men I'm consorted with."

Brimsey couldn't seem to think of any way to counter that point. He sank back in the seat in sullen silence.

"For now, your private life is not what's most important," he said after a few minutes. "Once this catastrophe is dealt with, I expect you to participate in some discussions with my department to ensure our society isn't compromised."

"Fine," I said. "I'll talk to your people."

It wasn't quite a victory, but at least the tension in the jeep felt a little less judgmental now.

Investigator Ruiz had been talking with someone on her phone. "We're coming up on the nearest observation point," she said, lowering the phone to her lap. "The creature should be in sight shortly."

The driver slowed the jeep as we ascended a low hill. Before we'd even reached its peak, a surge of unsettling energy wafted over me. The energy's off-kilter pulse raised the hairs on the back of my neck and made my stomach lurch. All at once, every nerve in my body screamed at me to run in the opposite direction.

Brimsey's hand tightened around the door handle. He might not have had any magical sensitivity of his own, but he was hardly numb to the demon's power.

I rubbed my arms, leaning forward to peer more intently out the windshield. We crested the hill, and the demon came into view.

I flinched at the sight of it, even though it was at least a quarter mile away still. A huge form was making its slow lurching way across a farmer's pasture. Even hunched over, its body was nearly as large as the delivery truck parked near the barn. A red-orange glow flowed over its skin, coiling and churning and never ceasing to move.

The thing traveled at a gait that was somewhere between a human crawl and an ape's knuckled lope, its features a similar mishmash of almost-human and animal and aspects that looked completely alien. Spikes with a metallic glint jotted from its curved back over a barrel chest. Its arms and legs bent in impossible ways. They each had an extra joint, I realized as nausea gripped my gut.

Its face was turned away from us, but the pitch-black eyes that had peered at me from the portal were burned into my memory clearly enough.

The dissonant energy the demon gave off had heightened in the air. My whole body had tensed against the urge to flee. When I managed to tear my gaze away from the creature, it settled on the patches of rotted vegetation left in the demon's path. Even as I watched, it hesitated for a moment, turning its head as if trying to get a read on the landscape around it, and the plants around it shriveled and grayed.

"Spark help us," Brimsey murmured. He'd seen the demon in the cave, but not out in the open like this, not until now. His face had completely blanched.

A farmhouse stood on the other side of the barn. A different sort of horror gripped me. "What about the people who live there? The demon must have crossed paths with some unsparked locals. If they start reporting it to their law enforcement and their news—"

"No one has reported it," Ruiz interrupted in a flat voice. "We've managed to evacuate most of the residents in its path so far. There haven't been many of them. I don't know how long the Assembly can keep up a story to divert them, but for now, it's been enough. And the power the demon gives off seems to make anyone traveling by turn away before they get close enough to see it." Her own hands were clenched on her knees, the knuckles white.

"You've evacuated *most*?" I repeated.

She wet her lips. "We weren't quite fast enough when it emerged. And in the middle of the night, at one point it changed directions abruptly, and we couldn't act in time... There have been five casualties so far."

Five deaths. Five innocent people dead, on top of all the witches whose lives had been ruined, thanks to the Frankfords and their faction's greed.

"There are two squads keeping watch," Ruiz went on with a motion of her hand. A gray sedan was parked near the top of another low hill beyond the farm. Another, this one black, was poised in the distance beyond the fields. "We have three other vehicles maintaining the evacuation."

"The locals are being taken to a community center in one of the nearby towns that we have access to," Brimsey said, with a waver to his words as he stared at the demon. "We're keeping them fed and looked after."

Right. As well as confused and away from their homes, while that thing left a path of destruction across their properties.

"What if it heads toward one of the towns near here?" I said. "We've been lucky so far that it's stayed in the less inhabited areas. We can't count on it remaining there forever."

"We'll do our best," Ruiz said, but her expression looked haunted.

"We're hoping we'll have a proper plan of action before it comes to that," Brimsey added. "Which is why we brought *you* in. Have you gotten any inspiration?"

He managed to sound like an ass even while he was terrified out of his wits. I might have turned to him with a sharp retort, but at that moment the demon's head swiveled toward us. My back went completely rigid.

Even across that distance, I felt those fathomless black eyes fix on the jeep. The erratic pulse of the energy warbled faster, making my skin twitch. For an instant, I was frozen, my lungs not even able to expand to draw breath. The flare of my spark inside my chest dulled.

I didn't have the power in me to turn back that thing. Not right now, not on my own.

As that realization washed over me, the demon

shifted its gaze again. I couldn't tell whether it had understood what the jeep was or that there were living people in it, but at the moment it didn't appear to care.

How long would this respite last? I swallowed hard, pushing myself straighter in the seat.

Every second that monster was still moving around freely out here, more people could die. More of our world was rotting in its wake. I might not be able to take it on now, but I'd find a way. I'd push it back into that portal or kill it and see the gate into their world sealed, no matter what I had to do.

There were no other options. Even if the man beside me and too many of his colleagues didn't see me as anything more than a miscreant.

"All right," I said, my nerves still jittering. "I've made my observations. Now let's head back and get that plan of action figured out before that thing gets any farther."

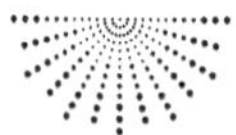

CHAPTER FOUR

Rose

By the time the jeep pulled up in front of the Assembly building, my stomach had just about settled. My thoughts were still spinning. How could we overcome the demon when so little of our magic could affect it? There had to be some kind of answer in the Frankfords' files. I knew Kyler and at least a couple of my other consorts were pouring over them again alongside the Assembly officials, but I figured I'd better add to those efforts.

When I stepped into the front hall, though, Gabriel and Seth were waiting for me. "Hey," Gabriel said, studying me. "How was it?"

I couldn't suppress the shudder that rippled through me. "Not good," I said, which was about as optimistic as I could manage to be. "It's killed people. It's destroying the land it crosses. We can't let it keep going."

"We won't," Seth said firmly. "It's just one demon. There are a whole lot of witches. We'll stop it."

"Yeah," I said, but just for a second all the bravado I'd been trying to hold onto fled. I stepped forward, reaching for both of my consorts, and they enveloped me in a joint hug. Their muscular frames, Seth's more broad and Gabriel's leaner, encircled me, and their combined scents—sweet and dark, warm and bronzy—filled my lungs.

What I'd said to Brimsey in the jeep was true. I *needed* these guys, for far more than to keep my spark lit. They steadied me.

They gave me all the reason I could ever require to fight my heart out.

Brimsey sighed as he stalked off, and I decided it was probably best to refrain from any overt PDAs here in the Assembly's office building. We were supposed to be here for business, after all. They'd take me and my consorts more seriously if we kept a somewhat professional attitude.

"Lady Ainsworth—Thalia—wanted you to come see her in the rooms where the recovering witches are staying," Gabriel said as he eased back. "The Assembly people brought in a few more of them this morning. She sounded like it was urgent—she was hoping to talk to you as soon as you got back."

My heart skipped a beat. Had something happened with the newly freed witches that Thalia didn't feel comfortable discussing with the Assembly? I could imagine they wouldn't be in a hurry to trust any of the officials when several of the members of the Frankfords' faction, including Charles Frankford, had been officials themselves.

"I'll go right now," I said. "Did she mention anything else?"

He shook his head and hesitated. "We'll come with you, if you think it'd be for the best."

"If our being there isn't going to upset anyone," Seth added. "Jin went by and did up protective tokens for the new arrivals, but he said some of them looked really shell-shocked."

"Why don't you come along and we'll see how it goes," I said. Gabriel's easy-going charm and Seth's stoic determination might be as comforting to the witches as Jin's playful good humor had been. "We still don't know everything they've been through. We'll just have to approach things cautiously."

Gabriel nodded. "If you think it's better for us to leave, just give the word."

We found Thalia in the same lounge room where I'd met with the first few recovering witches earlier. Nine of them were now sitting on the couches and chairs around the room, talking in hushed voices, their hands moving with nervous twitches. Thalia hurried to the doorway to meet us and ushered us back into the hall.

"What's the matter?" I said. "Is everyone okay?"

She gave me a tight smile. "As okay as they can be, after everything." Her own eyes were shining brighter than before, even more color back in her cheeks as her own recovery progressed. I could only imagine how much weight had been lifted off her with the removal of the spell that had kept her silent for so many years.

"That's what I wanted to talk to you about, though. I've been speaking with all of them as they've come in... They all understand the threat we're facing. And most of us agree that we have to do everything we can to defend against that fiend."

My gaze slid past her to the room behind her. "Of course. I mean, any information they can give that might be helpful, tactics we could use—as long as it doesn't strain them too much to talk about it. I know none of this has been easy for any of you."

"That's where I thought perhaps you could help," Thalia said. "We'd like to do even more than that if we can. At least a few of us would be willing to face those things again if it means we never have to fear them after that. But wanting to and being able to find the strength to... are not quite the same things. Your mind is clearer. Your magic hasn't been twisted the same way. And it's hard for us to turn to anyone in the Assembly in good faith. I'd like you to try guiding us through some joint healing exercises."

I balked instinctively. "I don't have that much practice at healing. I don't have that much practice at *anything* magical, really. I only came into my spark a few months ago."

And a few weeks ago, I'd been prepared to hurt anyone from the Frankfords' faction who came near me. I *had* hurt my former tutor trying to get information out of him. I'd gotten those darker impulses under control, but I still wasn't sure I should be trusted to heal people whose minds might be so fragile.

"It's all right," Thalia said, with a knowing look that

made me wonder how much of my doubt she understood. She'd been living in the Hallowell manor during the worst of that time—she might have overheard even more conversations than I knew. "I have some training in the healing arts. And this will be more mental than anything else. I can help direct you. I'm not sure we'll see a great effect very quickly, but over time—as much time as we have—I hope it'll make a difference."

"I suppose it can't hurt to try," I said, dragging in a breath. I glanced at the guys who'd accompanied me. "It sounds like maybe this is something that'll go over better if it's just us witches." It'd been the consorts of the witches in here who'd manipulated them, enslaved their magic. My consorts were strangers to them, but it might be hard for them to completely relax for a ritual like this in the presence of any men at all.

"That makes sense," Gabriel said. "I'm sure we can find some way to occupy ourselves that's at least a little bit useful."

He squeezed my hand, and Seth leaned in to give me a peck on the cheek. "I was thinking it'd be good to take a look at the demon's course on a map," the bigger guy started saying to the other as they headed off down the hall.

Thalia watched them go, her smile softening. "I wish my consort had held even half as much affection for me as yours clearly do for you."

I hadn't thought about the painful memories seeing us together might stir up for her too. "Now you're free of him," I said. "That's something, at least. And if you take that step again, you know it doesn't have to be with a witching man."

"Definitely a pertinent fact to keep in mind," she said wryly. Then she directed me back into the lounge room.

The witches looked up as we came back in, their expressions expectant. I got the impression that Thalia had already discussed her plan with all of them, and they'd just been waiting to see if I'd agree. They stood up from their seats, clustering around me with murmurs of gratitude and introductions from those I hadn't met before. A lump rose in my throat as I responded to a series of sentiments that could mostly be summed up as, "Thank you so much for what you did."

I was the one who'd exposed the Frankfords. It was thanks to me that these witches were freed from their awful duty. I'd been so caught up in worrying about the demon that the full impact hadn't quite sunk in until right now.

Maybe I did have it in me to truly heal.

As she'd promised, Thalia took the lead. "We should form a ring," she said, taking my hand in her smooth dry one. "As we soothe our sparks together, the healing energy can flow between all of us. We are stronger together, always."

Yes, I thought, the sentiment reverberating through me. It echoed the way I thought about my consorts so well.

The other witches shuffled into a loose circle. Crystal, the young witch with a sickly complexion who'd already been here early this morning, ended up at my other side. A little shiver ran from her into me as she wrapped her fingers around mine. From what I'd gathered, she'd consorted young, only eighteen years old, and her consort and father had pushed her involvement hard over the six years since. She was nearly as shaky as some of those who'd been drawn in decades ago.

"We've had so much taken from us, it's frightening to let any of our magic move through and out of us," Thalia said. "But it's only by releasing our magic that we can feel fulfilled in using it. It does no one any good keeping it bottled inside. Lady Hallowell will begin, just sending a touch of warmth through our circle. When you feel ready, add a little of your own. Let's find our way back to the witches we were meant to be."

I inhaled deeply, focusing on the warm glow of my spark inside me. It danced at my attention. With a gentle circling of my thumbs against the hands I held, I drew that warmth through my arms and urged it on into my companions. A soothing glow with nothing but kindness and compassion in it for these scarred but not broken women.

More warmth tickled against my palm from Thalia's hand as she tapped her forefinger to guide her own spell. The growing stream of it coursed through me and on toward Crystal. Another wash of it eased over me from the other side. And around the circle, the witches' faces were starting to relax. A glow lit in them too as they worked their magic without fear or compulsion.

A smile curved my lips. I *was* helping. Even if they could mostly thank Thalia's comments, her direction, my being here and starting the cycle had gotten them on the right path. Tremors of anxiety reached me here and there, but the warm glow quickly melted them away.

There could be a formidable force in this room, if we mended all the wounds these women had been dealt.

I wasn't sure how much time had passed before Thalia bowed her head. "I think that's a good start," she said. "We can't push recovery too quickly. You've all been very strong today. Thank you for standing with me."

"And thank you for standing with me," I added. I might not have been afraid of having the magic in me stolen, but this ritual had left me feeling even more centered, even more resolved.

"I'll talk with the others later this evening to see how they're feeling," Thalia told me as we moved back toward the door. "Maybe you could come back for something similar tomorrow. I know it means a lot to them just seeing you."

Suddenly I felt embarrassed again. "I didn't do that much. It was mostly you."

She shrugged. "We wouldn't be here at all if you hadn't found the strength to stand up to the Frankfords. None of us is ever going to forget that."

I swallowed hard. "I'll keep doing whatever I can, then," I said. "You're right. We're stronger together. And we're going to need an awful lot of strength to push that demon back."

CHAPTER FIVE

Kyler

I was so absorbed in scanning the words on the laptop's screen that I jumped in my chair at the click of the door. Rose peeked into the small office the Assembly had given to us.

"Hey," she said as she slipped inside. Her gaze found Seth where he'd ended up crashing on the sofa behind the desk about an hour ago, and her voice dropped lower to avoid waking him. "How's it going?"

"I'm seeing a lot of things," I said with a grimace. "I don't know if any of them are going to help us in our current situation. It seems like the Frankfords always figured that if the portal was compromised, they'd be around with their witch-slaves to fix it before anything got far. I've been taking notes of things that might be worth looking into further, though."

"Well, that's something." She came up beside me and

flicked one of the crumpled chip bags on the desk into the garbage can near the opposite chair.

"The mess is Damon's," I felt the need to say. "He managed to spend about half an hour looking through the records, which I think is about as long as he's capable of sitting in one place. He just went to grab us some takeout for dinner."

Rose frowned. "I'm sure if I ask one of the officials, they'll arrange a meal."

"I don't think any of us want to rely on your Assembly all that much," I said. "*Someone* here was authorizing the murders of witches who got too friendly with unsparked guys—someone had to be in the know about the real reason they were sending those enforcers after us before." They needed Rose right now, but I wasn't sure how much they thought they needed the rest of us.

"You don't think that person was swept up in the arrests they made?" Rose said.

I motioned to the computer screen. "There are some references to assistance, but no names given. I haven't seen anyone named who'd have that much authority in the Justice division of the Assembly, as far as I can tell."

Rose sighed and draped her arm across my shoulder. I leaned into her embrace, closing my eyes against the glow of the computer screen for a moment. Her lips brushed my forehead.

"I guess that's something for us to worry about when we don't have a demon on the loose. Have you gotten any sleep? It's been a long couple days."

"I got those few hours in the limo last night," I said.

"What about you? You've been running around all day—you went out and faced that thing."

"It's not really 'facing' it when you stay a quarter mile away," Rose muttered. "But hopefully we can really take it on soon and this will all be over."

I tugged her into my lap and took a deep breath of her sweet scent. She relaxed into me for a moment, resting her head on my shoulder.

"That'll be nice," I said. "When it's over, I mean. Everything's out in the open now, right? We can just... be consorts, without having to worry about keeping secrets."

"Yeah," Rose said. "I mean, we'll still have to be careful about how much we say to your families and everyone, not getting into the magical side of things... but yeah." She pressed her face to the side of my neck. "I'm sorry you've all gotten dragged into yet another witching mess."

"Hey." I squeezed her tighter, reveling in the softness of this body that I knew held so much power. "I wouldn't for a second take 'regular' life over getting to experience this. Sure, it's kind of scary, but what other unsparked guy ever got to delve into the real supernatural like this? It's fascinating to learn about when I'm not having to worry about my imminent death."

If the Assembly would let me have access to *all* their records after this was done... Man, I couldn't imagine all the crazy facts about magic and witching life I might be able to uncover.

"And it's not like I'd stand back and leave the saving the world just to you when I can pitch in," I added. "I live here too."

Rose let out a faint snort, but I thought she relaxed a little more at the same time. Then, with a reluctant expression, she eased herself upright on my lap.

"I actually came over for more than just a check-in," she said. "I managed to call together some of the main officials tonight so we can discuss our next steps. I think we need to talk to the members of the Frankfords' faction that have been arrested, to see if any of them are still holding onto some of that demonic power. Our magic doesn't seem to work so well against those things, but their own kind of power might."

"That makes sense," I said. "I've seen a couple of references in the files that make it sound like the guys who got the power put a little of it into keeping the portal sealed."

"That's exactly why I was hoping you'd come with me." Rose gave me a quick kiss. "You've read more of the records than anyone else. If I need back-up to convince them, it'd be great to have you there."

"Of course," I said, my heart lifting. To actually do something with the pieces I'd been putting together would be a welcome change. And if it proved to the Assembly that Rose hadn't been wrong to bring us into their community, all the better.

I grabbed the phone I'd been taking my notes on and went with Rose down the hall to the same meeting room where we'd spoken with the officials very early this morning.

A smaller group had gathered this time. Only Lady Northcott, not her husband as well, sat at the head of the table. Gwen Remington, Justin Brimsey, and the woman who'd spoken out against me and the other guys being there at all this morning had taken spots around the table too. The last woman, Lady Townsend, I'd gathered was someone pretty high up in the Justice division, so I guessed we weren't going forward with any plans without her approval any time soon. The investigator who'd helped Rose take down the Frankfords—Ruiz, I thought I'd heard—stood propped against the far wall.

It made me feel a little more sure on my feet just knowing the names of everyone in the room this time around.

"I didn't think you'd gleaned much from your trip this afternoon," Townsend said, looking as severe as ever as she glowered at Rose. "Have you made some kind of urgent discovery that we have to know about immediately? Or maybe you think one of your consorts has?" Her gaze slid to me, her tone as she said the word *consorts* turning acidic.

Rose didn't bother sitting down. She stopped at the edge of the table and crossed her arms over her chest. "Not an urgent discovery but an urgent request. Seeing the demon up close out there only reinforced my understanding of how powerful it is. We're going to need every edge we can get against it. And I think the best edge we have access to is to turn its own kind of power against it. The Assembly has taken all of the members of the Frankfords' faction that you could locate into custody, haven't you?"

"We have," Lady Northcott said cautiously.

"I'd like permission to interview them," Rose said. "And permission to use a truth compulsion spell to confirm whether they're telling the truth about what powers they might still hold. Or else send an enforcer with me to do that part. We just need to know as soon as possible."

"Now, hold on," Townsend spoke up before anyone else could. She leaned her knobby elbows onto the tabletop. "This group of witching folk clearly broke laws, and they were playing with something they didn't fully understand and should have known they couldn't control. But I'm not convinced they were manipulating anyone so much as being manipulated themselves by those creatures. I'm definitely not convinced they got any real power from them—the kind of magic they could keep lit over all this time like a spark."

"I witnessed it with my own eyes when Charles Frankford used some sort of magic-like power against Lady Hallowell," Remington said. "He'd kept that energy inside him at least as long as it'd been since he'd last interacted with the fiends. He admitted that he and his allies drew power from the creatures."

"Or maybe the power came from the demons nearby immediately in that moment," Townsend said. "You were on his property, close to this cave where they called them forth. The rest could easily have been a delusion constructed by the creatures to further their own ends."

I couldn't help breaking in. "Why do you think it's more likely that they were deluded than that they really were collecting power?" I asked. Why was she so intent on downplaying their responsibility?

"It doesn't even matter," Rose said, her jaw set. "We can find out what's real easily enough if we talk to them.

If they're compelled to tell the truth, there'll be ways to fully confirm their stories."

"Truth compulsion is only meant to be used under select circumstances where the proof of necessity is immense," Townsend protested. "Even a carefully crafted spell of that sort can have lingering effects on the mind. These people may be criminals, but they still have some rights."

Okay, now she was just being ridiculous. "How much proof do you need?" I asked. This was exactly why Rose had wanted me here. I waved my phone, which could have connected me to those files in an instant. "There are a whole bunch of records that mention ways these people were able to affect things, nowhere near the demons, that they shouldn't have been able to do without some special power."

"The power of a delusion—"

I talked right over her. "There's the guy who managed to persuade a politician to pick his company for a contract from the other side of the restaurant they were both in—a contract other documents suggest the politician had been set to give to someone else. And the guy who shoved one of his business competitors through a window without even being in the same room as him, just watching via security camera footage. Do I need to bring up more examples? I can draw you some flow charts if it'll help. There's a lot more than some delusion going on there."

Townsend's mouth opened and closed and opened again, but she couldn't seem to work any words out. Before she managed to, Lady Northcott spoke up.

"Both Lady Hallowell and her consort have made a convincing case. I believe we should move forward with this line of inquiry."

Townsend's mouth clamped tight. She shot a glare at Rose that made no sense to me at all. The back of my neck prickled. She seemed awfully invested in this discussion for someone who should have been most concerned about stopping that demon thing from hurting anyone else. Wasn't she supposed to stand for justice?

"Perhaps Investigator Ruiz can oversee the questioning," Lady Northcott went on, with a glance toward the enforcer. "Lady Townsend, we'll want at least two other enforcers present, to witness the correct conduct of any truth compulsion used and, well, because we can't be entirely sure how these accused will react."

Townsend's lips pursed. "I'll need to confirm the allocation with the head of Justice."

Northcott gave her a puzzled look. "*I* give you the authority to make that call right now. We don't have time to waste. I want them ready first thing in the morning." She rubbed her jaw, a momentary weariness showing in her eyes.

Townsend's comment stuck in my head. *Confirm the allocation.* Why did that sound so familiar?

My memories of the last several hours of research raced through my head. I'd seen that wording somewhere in the files, hadn't I?

Yes. In a record mentioning some event where one of the faction members had planned to work some kind of scheme, where they'd wanted a few enforcers in attendance. There'd been a note about how an Assembly contact would need to "confirm the allocation." It'd seemed like weird phrasing to me, and I hadn't seen them use it anywhere else in their comments. Which suggested it hadn't been their wording but the contact's.

Between her weird behavior and that specific phrase, a sudden certainty gripped me. My back tensed, but I made myself look straight at Lady Townsend. "You were the one in the Justice division who helped the Frankfords out when they needed Assembly support, weren't you?" We wouldn't even get into the murders she might have helped orchestrate.

She clearly hadn't been expecting that accusation. Her pinched features flinched before she schooled her expression back into her usual disapproving look. "What is your unsparked partner ranting about now, Lady Hallowell?" she said, cold and crisp.

I wasn't going to let her dismiss me like that. "You're doing everything you can to take the blame away from these witching people, to make it sound as if every crime they committed was the demons' fault," I said. "And you don't want us to question them—because you're worried someone who knows about you will end up mentioning your name? What you just said about 'confirming the allocation,' that's something you said to the Frankfords before. They recorded it just the way you said it in their files, you know."

Lady Northcott had turned toward Townsend, her mouth pressing into a flat line. "You have been raising a rather unusual number of concerns given the dire situation we've found ourselves in. Can you offer any other explanation for why you've been protecting these known criminals over the innocents the demon might harm?"

Lady Townsend started to sputter. "I simply— Our people's rights must be considered—"

Rose's eyes narrowed. "We know for sure there's someone in the Assembly the Frankfords had help from. It had to be someone who could make decisions in the Justice Division."

"This is absurd," Townsend spat out. She turned to Lady Northcott. "I can't believe you'd accept an accusation like this from a—"

Northcott made a gesture with her hand, so brief and small I almost missed it. Investigator Ruiz moved at once. Her fingers twitched as she swiveled her wrist, calling a spell into being.

"Lady Veronica Townsend, by the order of the authority of the Assembly and in this state of near-emergency, you will answer the next question truthfully."

Her voice crackled with the same sort of power I'd heard in Rose's on occasion. Townsend stiffened. Brimsey stepped forward behind her as if to cut her off if she meant to make a run for it.

"Did you assist Charles Frankford in any of his illicit dealings?" Lady Northcott said tersely.

Townsend's mouth twisted. "Yes," she said, as if the admission had been wrenched out of her. "I did." She gasped as the spell must have loosed its hold. "You have to understand. I wasn't fully aware—"

Northcott's face had hardened. "We can discuss that

in preparation for your hearing. Investigator, please take her to a holding room."

When the traitor had left the room, I let out my breath, my chest tight. Lady Northcott's shoulders bowed as she leaned her hands on the table.

"All right," she said, sounding even wearier than before. "I think that's enough for one night." She looked to me. "Thank you for your quick observations." And then to Rose. "You'll have the support you need early tomorrow morning. In the meantime, I think we'd all better get some rest. That creature is moving slowly now. If that changes, we won't be any match for it at all if we're already exhausted."

CHAPTER SIX

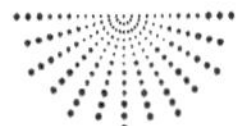

Rose

Lady Northcott had pretty much ordered us to sleep. Unfortunately my mind didn't take those kind of orders easily. The sleep I did get was strung through with dreams of that unearthly demon form turning its massive head toward me and the world around me crumbling into dry rot. I woke up more than once with sweat sticky on my skin.

The third or fourth time, there was just enough near-dawn light seeping through the room's one small window that I could make out the other cots the Assembly had arranged for us in this makeshift dorm room. I hadn't wanted to be separated from any of my consorts overnight, and we'd wanted to be close at hand where the Assembly could reach out to us in case the demon changed tactics all at once, so we hadn't gotten a whole lot of choice in our bedroom situation.

The guys were all sprawled on their respective cots, the rising and falling rasp of sleeping breaths filling the room. Except for the cot at my right—Gabriel's. It was empty other than a tangle of sheet and blanket.

My pulse hiccupped. I sat up, the sweat on my arms turning cold.

He wouldn't have left. He'd sworn he'd never really wanted to leave us in the first place. I couldn't imagine any reason why he'd do that now.

But my heart still thumped a little too quickly as I eased out of the room. The sound of fingers pattering over a keyboard reached me from the office the Assembly had set up for us on the opposite side of the hall.

My nerves settled as I pushed open that door and found Gabriel frowning at the screen of the laptop Damon had been using earlier. He edged back his chair at the squeak of the hinges and gave me a smile that didn't quite erase the worry from his gaze.

"Hey, Sprout," he said, opening his arms to me. "Up already?"

"I should be saying that to you," I said as I let myself sink into his lap. I looped my arm loosely around his neck. "I woke up and you weren't there."

"Oh, shit, I'm sorry," he said before I had to explain any more than that. He hugged me close. "I didn't mean to worry you. I'd just been tossing and turning for an hour, figured if I was going to be awake anyway, I might as well try to do something useful with that time."

I peered at the computer screen, the glow harsh on my still-tired eyes. "Did you find anything you think will help?"

He shook his head. "I've got to admit I'm not even totally sure what I should be looking for. My searching has been kind of aimless. Not much better than nothing. I wish I could figure out a way to help more than this."

He sounded so overwhelmed in that moment that my heart squeezed. I touched the side of his face, drawing it closer to mine.

"You're helping plenty," I said. "You help just by being here. We're stronger together, and I'm so much stronger because I have you. Don't you ever forget that."

Gabriel cupped my cheek and kissed me in answer. As his mouth moved against mine, a pang of longing shot through me, for this closeness I hadn't gotten to really enjoy with any of my consorts in the last stressful few days. Even the last time Gabriel and I had come together, it'd been more about healing some of the wounds our relationship had be dealt, not simple enjoyment and passion.

When had anything between the six of us ever gotten to be simple? *Would* it ever be?

As if he'd read my thoughts, Gabriel pulled back from me, just far enough to speak. "I don't care what any of those officials think, Rose. I don't care what any of them say. This is *right*. This is where I'm meant to be—where we're all meant to be. They can take their prejudices and shove them where the sun don't shine."

A laugh escaped me, and then I was kissing him again, with more hunger than before. Yes, this was right. Right, the way our breaths blended together. Right, the heat of his tongue teasing over mine. Right, the tingling of my skin as his hands eased up my sides.

The longing swelled into a need. I shifted myself on the chair to straddle him. Gabriel gripped my waist, watching me for a cue but with eyes lit with desire. I drew a flicker of my spark to my fingertips with a twist of my wrist and spelled the door's lock into place.

I didn't want any officials walking in on us—but they couldn't tell us that the love we were about to make wasn't valid.

I'd worn a loose dress to bed in case I was woken and had to spring into action in a hurry, but I hadn't bothered with a bra underneath. Gabriel's thumbs traced the curves of my breasts and stroked my nipples into pebbles. I whimpered, rocking against him. Our kisses turned sloppy as he eased up my dress and eased down my panties. I fumbled with his fly, my urgency growing as he slicked his hand over the ready folds between my legs.

When he pushed into me, I held him there for the first few seconds, just reveling in the sensation of being filled, of being connected in every possible way. "I love you," I murmured.

"God, Rose, I love you too," Gabriel said, his voice ragged. He tugged me down for another kiss as we began to buck together toward our release. Each pump of his cock inside me echoed the eager thump of my heart. And when I came, my consort following me just moments later, our cries twined together in perfect harmony.

If this wasn't right, then there couldn't be anything in the world that was.

* * *

I was supposed to meet Investigator Ruiz in the front hall at eight am, and I made it there on time and with all my clothes in order, even though I'd ended up falling back asleep cuddled up with Gabriel on the office couch. The enforcer turned toward me with a faint smile.

"We may need to wait a few minutes before we head over to the Assembly's holding building," she said. "The other enforcers assigned to this case will meet us there, but I'm expecting someone whose presence might benefit us."

My eyebrows rose. "Who's that?" I asked. And then I didn't need Ruiz to answer, because a young woman in a crisply tailored suit walked through the front doors.

"Rose," Caroline Almeida said hesitantly. Her face looked paler than the last time I'd seen her, any make-up on it only the remains of yesterday's, and her shiny blond hair was rumpled.

Caroline was the daughter of two of my father's close colleagues—two of the Frankfords' close colleagues too—and our last conversation had been when she'd dropped by my estate to see if I could tell her what schemes they might have been getting up to. I hadn't been able to offer much information at the time. I guessed she'd gotten a whole lot of answers in the last day and a half.

"Hi," I said, feeling equally hesitant. I couldn't imagine how she was feeling right now—about her parents, about the whole crazy situation, or about me. I'd *wanted* to warn her. The oath I'd taken with Frankford had prevented me. But emotions weren't exactly logical. She might be upset that I hadn't told her more anyway.

She twined her hands in front of her, her posture

awkwardly stiff. "I—I got into town last night. I heard what was happening, and I had to do something, especially knowing my parents were wrapped up in all this somehow..." She bit her lip. "Lady Northcott told me what you were planning to try this morning. She thought it might help you with some of the prisoners if I tagged along for the interviews. I might know some of them better, the ones who were closer to my family than yours."

"Of course," I said, relaxing a little. "That makes sense. We were just about to head out."

Caroline kept worrying at her lip as Ruiz escorted us to the Assembly sedan waiting outside. "I talked with some of the other witches here last night," the young witch said once we'd slid inside. "The ones these people used. They're so—it's like they're missing something. Like something was taken from them, or they were broken somehow..."

"They're not broken," I said with a fierceness I hadn't realized I'd feel. I willed myself calmer. "They just need time to heal."

"Oh, I know, I didn't mean—" She winced, ducking her head. "I just can't help thinking it could have been me too. Maybe my parents would have roped me into that. I don't know what they were planning. I never would have thought... I should probably stay back when you question *them*, because I don't know how I'll react, but I want to hear what they say."

A twinge of sympathy ran through my chest. I touched her arm briefly. "I get it. I know what it's like, finding out your parents aren't who you thought they were."

I'd spent so much time torn up wondering what my father's intentions for me were, whether he could really have meant to carry out such an enormous betrayal after what had seemed like a loving childhood... My throat tightened.

I shook those thoughts away, but stepping into the holding building sent an uneasy jitter down my spine. I'd been here once before—when my consorts and I had been held in those little white rooms for interrogation. The sight of the bland hallways and the faint ozone smell in the air made my stomach turn. I clenched my jaw, girding myself.

Maybe I should get the hardest part of this task over with first, before I'd been worn down by this place, by the conversations I was going to have to carry out. As three more enforcers joined our little cluster, I turned to Ruiz.

"I want to interview my father first."

She studied me with her dark eyes. "Are you sure?"

"He's been close with the Frankfords for a long time," I said. "I'd bet he got more power from their awful rituals than most of their allies did." Whether he still had any of it at his command, we'd just have to find out.

"This way, then." She motioned for us to follow. We went up a flight of stairs and partway down another familiar hallway. One of the other enforcers unlocked the door.

My father was sitting on the padded bench across from the doorway. It was the only furniture in the room. His clothes, which I guessed he'd been wearing since he'd been taken in, were wrinkled, and his face looked drawn. I noticed with mild satisfaction that his hands had been padded and chained like mine had been.

Townsend might have been sowing doubt about how much power the witching men in this faction could have wielded, but the Assembly had taken every precaution anyway.

"Rose," Dad said, staring, his voice somehow hopeful and apprehensive at the same time.

"I'd prefer Lady Hallowell from now on," I said in the most even voice I could summon. "I have just a few questions for you. One of the enforcers will put you under a truth compulsion to ensure you answer truthfully."

"What? I—"

"Under the approval of the Northcotts," Ruiz said, and nodded to one of the other enforcers. The other witch wove her fingers through the air to draw the intricate spellwork into being.

Dad stiffened as she cast her magic toward him. The tendons along his jaw flexed.

"We're going to talk about the magic-like power the demons gave some of your faction in exchange for being 'fed' by the witches you trapped," I said. "Did you ever take any of that power into yourself?" No point in beating around the bush. I wanted to spend as little time as possible in the company of the man who'd planned to essentially sell my soul.

Dad's shoulders sagged in what looked like resignation. "Yes," he said in a dull voice. "I did."

"Do you have any of that power in you now?"

"No. It's been quite some time. We can't handle very much of it at once, for it to last us beyond one or two acts."

I should have been glad that he was cooperating so well, telling me more than I'd asked, but my gut twisted. If the demon conspirators couldn't hold onto very much power, that meant there was less chance that we'd find any of the witching men who hadn't used anything they'd taken in already.

"Do you know who in your group most recently absorbed that power?" I asked.

He shook his head. "Charles did, frequently," he said. "But I don't know for sure when last. The others— we usually came separately."

Charles had used his last bit of demonic energy trying to kill me.

"All right," I said, relieved that the interview could end here even if I was disappointed not to have learned more. "I'm sure others will be back to ask more questions when the current emergency is dealt with."

The enforcer motioned to dispel the truth compulsion. Dad's head jerked up. He stared at me again, but this time his eyes were frantic. "That's all? The demon—Rose, with it on the loose, you have to— You're our best hope of controlling it."

Was he telling the truth or guilting me with more lies? Did it even matter? I was already here, already doing whatever I could.

"You're not going to make this my fault for not submitting to being a demon's meal," I said, unable to completely keep the edge out of my voice.

"If there's something specific you can think of that might help us bring it under control," Ruiz said, "report it to us immediately, as you've been told." The enforcers must have done an initial round of questioning on that subject, as soon as the demon had made its appearance.

Dad slumped back against the wall, clearly with nothing else to add. I turned to the enforcers and Caroline, who was watching me with wide eyes.

"Fine," I said. "Let's move on to the next one."

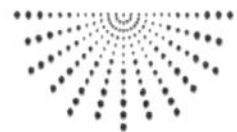

CHAPTER SEVEN

Rose

"So you're just going to go out there and face off against this thing?" Damon demanded. "With no one but a bunch of these Assembly idiots backing you up?"

"They're not all idiots," I said, but I had to cut him a little slack for his frustration. Out of all the guys, Damon had the hardest time staying cooped up. "And that's not all we've got. A couple of the men from the Frankfords' faction were still holding a little of the demon's power. There'll be a bunch of enforcers there to keep them in line and help amplify that power to push back the demon."

"And then what?" Kyler asked from the desk, where he'd turned away from the laptop. We were all gathered in our little office.

I was less sure about that part of the plan, mostly because I wasn't completely sure the first part was going to work. "Well, if it all goes well, we push the demon all the way back to the Cliff and force it back through the portal. Then we seal the portal and close off the cave—permanently, if we can."

Jin gave me an unusually serious look. "The other witches—they said they had to use *blood* to keep the portal secure."

I wet my lips. We'd heard the same story from the faction members, under much duress. A bodily sacrifice gave the magic maintaining the portal a certain power. Unfortunately—or fortunately, depending on how you looked at it—they'd all agreed that similar techniques weren't likely to do us much good against the demon now that it was out on our plane. *The sacrifice works to add power to one spell, one spot,* one had put it. *An ongoing effort... You'd all bleed yourselves dry.*

He hadn't looked exactly sad about that idea.

"If we can get it through the portal, we'll do what we have to do," I said. "The witches the faction used have been making that sacrifice for years. I'll happily spill a little of my blood if it means we never have to worry about those creatures again."

Damon shoved himself off the couch, his hands clenched. "You shouldn't have to do it alone. I'll come with you." He glanced around at the other guys with a glower that seemed to dare them not to make the same offer.

"Hey," I said, stepping closer to him and taking his hand. "I know how badly you want to be part of the fight, but I don't think it's a good idea. This is going to be all magic, from start to finish—and a bigger magic than I could send into some baton for you to use. I'll be able to focus on driving the demon back so much easier if I know you're safe back here and not in its attack range."

Damon looked as if he were going to argue. I squeezed his hand. "Please. If this goes the way the Assembly is hoping... we might be able to go home tonight."

He made a disgruntled sound, but he settled for giving me a quick but intent kiss. The rest of my consorts embraced me one by one. Gabriel pressed his lips to my forehead before he let me go.

"We'll see you when you get back," he said firmly, neither his tone nor his expression betraying any doubt that I *would* make it back.

I didn't really like leaving them behind, as much as I would have hated to bring them within reach of the demon. Even a few hours later, as a jeep carried Thalia, Caroline, and me out to the fiend's current location, my stomach stayed knotted tight, apprehensive about both the battle ahead and my consorts' fates.

How safe *were* they in the Assembly building? We'd uncovered Lady Townsend's treachery, but she might have had other allies, people who were against the mingling of witches with the unsparked.

I'd asked the guys to stick together. And I'd also asked Investigator Ruiz if she could arrange that at least one enforcer she trusted could be keeping an eye on our rooms while I was gone, just in case.

Thalia's knuckles had turned white where her hands

were clasped in her lap. She'd come out to the Cliff with us when we'd exposed the Frankfords, but she hadn't seen one of the demons since whenever her husband had last let them feed off her magic. She'd insisted on joining us even though none of the other recovering witches had been able to consider the idea.

"Are you going to be all right?" I asked her.

"I feel better taking it on than cowering back in my room," she said. "But... it's going to be difficult holding my ground. I don't blame the others for not being up to it yet. I'll make sure I'm not in anyone's way if I have to retreat."

"I guess I should say the same," Caroline said at my other side. "The best I might be able to do is stand back and offer the boost of my magic to anyone who needs it."

"That's mostly how I'll be contributing too," I said. "The enforcers have a lot more training in offensive and defensive magic than I do." I nodded to the witches at the front of the jeep.

But I had plenty of magic at my disposal. My spark was blazing brightly in my chest, barely used since I'd come out to help the Assembly. If I could make the difference between this plan succeeding and it not, I wanted to be here.

The demon's unnatural energy wavered into the air around us and quivered down to my bones. I rubbed my arms against the crawling of my skin. Caroline shuddered, and Thalia's shoulders stiffened.

"If it looks half as horrible as it feels," Caroline murmured, and then she didn't need to finish that sentence, because we came around a treed bend into view of the creature itself.

The demon was still taking a slow exploratory route across the farmlands and forests in this isolated section of the state. At least that part of the Frankfords' plan—setting up their portal where no one was likely to stumble on it—had worked to our advantage. Right now, the monster was moving with its lurching gait across a meadow spotted with trees. As we watched, it tested its massive clawed hand against one. The way its mouth twisted in apparent gratification at the sagging of the rotted branches made me queasy.

The cars in front of us pulled off onto the sides of the road. Our driver followed suit. We clambered out alongside several dozen enforcers and the two men from the Frankfords' faction.

"Everyone in the positions we agreed on," the sergeant in charge hollered, managing to pitch her voice so it wouldn't travel too far across the field. "Cautious with the approach. Begin the push on my signal."

Thalia stuck with me, as we'd agreed on back during our strategy meeting. Another squad of enforcers moved off with Caroline. The older witch and I and the eight enforcers who made up our squad marched with cautious but steady footsteps into the tall grass. The blades rustled against our calves. The delicate smell of wildflowers rising from the patches here and there might have been comforting if a prickle of decay hadn't reached my nose from the demon's path.

The squads who were escorting the men gathered in front of us. We were coming up beside the creature. Its path had been winding, and we didn't need to push it straight back, just to the left of the way it'd been going, to get it back toward its "home."

The demon's head turned toward us, and the sergeant waved for us to stop in our tracks. My heart thudded as those opaque eyes scanned our ranks. There was nothing but malevolence in them now.

It started to swing its hunched body toward us, and the sergeant jerked her hand again. We were only about fifty feet away now—we'd have to hope that was close enough, because if we waited any longer, there was no telling what it might do to us first.

My arms lifted into the air, twining and releasing as I summoned the energy from my spark and cast it out toward the enforcers ahead of me. All of them were moving too. Their bodies swayed in sync with each other through practiced magical forms, with a few new twists to account for this unusual strategy. The two men who'd joined us stretched their hands out in front of them, palms toward the demon.

It's through the palms, one of the faction members I'd talked to yesterday had told me. *I don't know why. That's how we take it in, and how we let it back out.*

A different sort of hum dispersed the unnatural quivering in the air around us. It was a warbling of our own magical energy that the great Spark had blessed witching kind with, as much a part of me as the thump of my pulse and the strands of my hair now tossed by the wind. Tremors of that dissonance ran through the wave of magic from the men, but mostly away from me, toward the demon. Only a hint of it touched my body.

The first rush of power smacked into the demon just as it had finished swinging toward us. It flinched, and the reddish glow on its hazy skin wavered. The enforcers swiveled on their feet, moving even faster. With a hollow-sounding groan, the demon shuffled back one pace and then another. Its already gnarled face contorted into a grimace.

It was working. My spirits leapt. I pushed my own gestures faster, urged my own spark higher and hotter, pouring all the magic I could summon toward those who could shape it best.

The demon scuttled backward another few steps. Then its back arched. A flash of panic shot through me in the instant before it lunged at us.

The sweep of its clawed fingers propelled a shrieking wave of its awful energy into us. The blast rocked me on my feet. Thalia let out a cry, falling to her knees. The enforcers near the front of the assault stumbled, many of them falling to their knees.

"Regroup, regroup!" the sergeant shouted. "We had it. Push back—push harder. Encircle it."

The squads ahead of us spread out in a semi-circle around the creature. Their arms lashed through the air, and their feet stamped against the ground. I threw myself into another round of magicking, my breath sharp in my throat. We had to get that control back. We'd managed to move the demon a little. If we could just keep that effort up—

But the creature didn't even wince this time. Its head swiveled on its thick neck as it took in our scramble around it. Its black eyes gleamed. Thalia stayed crouched on the ground, but I forced myself to walk closer to the edge of the circle, where I could continue passing on my magic most effectively.

I'd just come up a few feet behind the front lines, the rest of my squad around me, when the demon's gaze jerked straight to me. Its fathomless gaze fixed on my face with an attention that crept through every nerve in my body. My feet lost their rhythm; the sway of my arms faltered.

The monster leaned forward as if studying me, and that horrible smile I'd seen when it had rotted the tree stretched across its face again. The witches between me and it were casting more spells, but the demon barely seemed to notice. I staggered backward, unable to tear my gaze from its inhuman eyes. The intensity of its focus gripped me as tightly as if it'd closed its claws around me. My thoughts jittered. Was it trying to tear right into my mind?

No. I concentrated on my spark, on the heat and the glow of life inside me. My magic flowed through my limbs and over my skin.

The demon made a sound like a groaned snarl. Its claws whipped out, smacking into the front line of enforcers. One speared a witch right through the skull. Another sprawled on the ground, her legs streaming blood.

"Retreat!" the sergeant called out. I caught sight of her for an instant before the surge of the squads swept me up. Her face was bloodless, even her lips near-white.

I whirled and dashed toward Thalia, who was struggling to her feet on the field behind me. But even as we ran, the demon's eyes bored into my back. I felt it tracking me, niggling at my mind, from the moment my hand closed around the older witch's elbow, all the way back to the jeep, and through the screeching of tires as we fled.

CHAPTER EIGHT

Damon

I was trying to be patient, but every man has his limits. I'd poked at the second computer in our rinky-dink office for a while, peered at the maps Seth was making notations I didn't totally understand on, and went out to grab us coffees and then lunch at places nearby that had nothing to do with the Assembly. But even walking on the streets of downtown Portland outside wasn't enough to distract me.

Rose was out there fighting that... that *thing* that had practically made me piss myself just looking at it through the portal a month ago, and I was stuck here playing food delivery boy.

Not that I thought I'd really be all that much use out there on the battlefield either. If I would have been, I'd have argued a hell of a lot more. The last thing I wanted to be was a liability to her. So delivery boy it was.

In the middle of the afternoon, I stalked down the hallway to peer out the streaky window there. A car honked on the road below. There was still no sign of the witches who'd headed out en masse this morning. No sign of Rose. If the Assembly officials still dicking around here pretending *they* were so useful knew anything, they hadn't bothered to keep us in the loop.

I had people I could talk to who knew other people. I could have scrounged up some guns or maybe other types of handheld weaponry. The pistol I'd gotten in New York hadn't helped us much against even the Enforcers, though. And during that first meeting, the Assembly assholes had mentioned that their enforcers had tried a certain amount of non-magical firepower against the demon. Bullets had bounced right off its freakish skin. It figured.

When I wandered back into the office, Kyler and Gabriel barely looked up from their respective computers. Jin and Seth were sitting on the couch together discussing something about "angles" and "patterning," like they were going to crochet their way out of this problem.

I'd just dropped onto the end of the couch beside them when one of the officials—that Brimsey guy who always got an expression like he'd bitten into a bruise on an apple when he looked at us—peeked in at us as he meandered by down the hall.

In what was not quite my finest moment, a comment shot from my mouth before I had a chance to think. "We're not here for you to gawk at. If you've got some news, spit it out."

His mouth tightened, and he strode off without a word. Brilliant strategy, Damon. Way to win them over.

But let's be real. Winning people over was Gabriel's job, and maybe Jin's. Mine was to stop them from getting away with bullshit.

True to form, our recently returned leader shifted in his chair to look at me. "I think we're better off giving them at least a little benefit of the doubt," Gabriel said.

"I think he'll survive the occasional jab," I said.

He shrugged. "I hate them too. Hate them all you want. I just figure we'll have an easier time when we leave here if we keep the peace while we're with them."

The most annoying thing about Gabriel was that he almost always had a good point. I scuffed my feet against the floor with a scowl. I was supposed to be keeping the peace with *him* too, even though he'd taken off on all of us after stomping Rose's heart to pieces. Even if he'd left for good reasons in the end, it'd still gotten stomped on.

She was the one who'd asked me to keep the peace, though. I could do that for her.

Ky glanced over too. "Why don't—" he started, but before I could find out what our Brainiac was going to suggest I occupy myself with, a scramble of footsteps sounded in the hall outside.

We all jumped up. I made it to the doorway first. A few of the Assembly officials farther down the hall were hurrying to the staircase. Something was up.

I didn't wait to discuss it—I hustled right after them. The other guys kept pace. We rushed down the stairs and spilled into the front hall just behind the officials.

The enforcers who'd left that morning were coming

in. The bunch I saw was clustered around one woman who was limping, her mouth twisted with pain. I caught sight of another witch with a blotch of eerie gray across her cheek as if the skin had rotted. My stomach lurched.

Where the hell was Rose? What had that fucking fiend done to *her*?

Her black hair gleamed between two of the enforcers just coming through the doors to join the crowd in the hallway. I leapt forward, pushing through the chaos as gently but quickly as I could. In the space of a breath, I took in my consort's face—paler than usual but unharmed—and her posture—all body parts apparently in working order, if weak. Then I pulled her into my arms.

She hugged me back, her fingers digging into the fabric of my T-shirt. Her breath came out ragged. A quiver ran down her back, and my teeth gritted.

The other guys had caught up. "Is she okay?" Seth asked.

I nodded. At Gabriel's gesture, I eased both Rose and me back against the wall, farther out of the way of the enforcers still streaming into the building. Babbling voices echoed around us, but there was only one person's account I really cared about.

"What happened, angel?" I said. It hadn't been good —that much I could tell.

"I don't know," she said against my chest. "I don't really understand... The plan didn't work. Not completely. We started to push the demon back, but even with all of us there, it was stronger. And I think we made it mad."

A chill coursed down my back. All those enforcers and Rose and the best plan they'd come up with, and the demon hadn't even been slowed down. What was it going to do now that they'd shown their hand?

"There've got to be other things we can try," Jin said, trying to put an optimistic spin on the situation as always. "If you found a strategy that worked a little, you can build off of that."

"I hope so," Rose said. She raised her head a bit, but she sounded doubtful. Her eyes were so distraught that my heart wrenched. "That wasn't even—"

"Lady Hallowell!" One of the officials who'd set themselves up in charge from the beginning—Remington —pushed over to us through the crowded hall. She motioned toward the stairwell. "We need to talk about what happened out there. As soon as possible."

Rose nodded and raised her chin as she moved toward the stairwell. The rest of us followed her—what else was there for us to do?

In the meeting room upstairs, the two Northcotts who apparently *really* ran things around here and a couple of the other officials from before were standing around the table, along with a few witches in enforcer sweat suits. No one sat down even after we filed into the room.

Rose came to a stop behind one of the chairs, her brow knitting as she looked around at the people gathered there. I stayed right beside her, as close as I thought she'd be okay with in front of these spectators. She shouldn't have to feel ashamed if she needed to lean on someone after what she must have been through in that battle, but even I knew this wasn't the moment to force the issue.

The three enforcers looked tired and a little wary, but the officials' stances were practically rigid. What were they so tense about? And why were they focused on Rose? They weren't blaming her for the plan not working out, were they? They'd all agreed to it. It'd been better than anything these assholes had come up with alone. I didn't have to be there to know Rose had tried her best to see it through.

"We understand the attempt at magnifying the residual stored demon power to repel the intruder had some initial success, but quickly lost efficacy," Mr. Northcott said, setting one hand on the table. "Is that also your impression, Lady Hallowell?"

Rose gazed back at him with the same puzzled expression. "Yes. I'm sure anyone who was there could tell you that."

"And to what would you attribute that loss of efficacy?" Lady Northcott asked. If anything, her posture had gotten even more stiff.

"The residual power, or our amplification of it, mustn't have been strong enough," Rose said. "My best guess would be that we were able to overcome the demon's will at first, when we took it by surprise and were at our freshest, but it took a lot of effort. We tired, and it adapted to what we were doing. I mean, that's what makes the most sense."

The dour expressions around the table suggested that the officials didn't think so, even though the enforcers were nodding in agreement.

"There was something odd, though," Rose went on. "Right before it started attacking, the demon seemed to be focused on me, or something around me... I don't know how to explain it." She rubbed her mouth with an anxious twitch of her hand.

Lady Northcott's eyebrows rose. "And you didn't do anything to provoke that interest?"

Rose blinked at her. "Of course not. I wasn't even on the front line. I stayed behind most of the enforcers, sending all the energy from my spark that I could forward to them, as we discussed. Did someone say I stepped out of my place?"

Remington ignored that question. "Where exactly did you get the idea for this plan to make use of the men who might hold demon power in the first place, Lady Hallowell?"

Rose turned to her, even more bewildered than before. "What does that have to do with anything? It was just something that occurred to me after what I saw and knowing what I do about how the Frankfords' and their faction worked. You all told me none of our usual magic had affected it much. It seemed reasonable to think the powers of its own world might have more impact."

"I think we need a step by step rundown of everything you recall doing from the moment you set off with the Justice force," Lady Northcott said.

Rose's mouth tightened, but she launched into a recitation of the drive out, the way she'd hung right at the back at first and then moved forward as the squads spread out. Her hands balled against the top of the chair back as she talked. To stop them from shaking, I realized, when a tremble slipped through anyway.

My jaw clenched. She was upset about what had happened—that encounter with the demon had obviously shaken her up—and these pricks were practically interrogating her.

They didn't look any happier when she finished. "During the period when you moved closer to the demon, did you change the way you were casting your spell at all?" Remington said.

"No," Rose said. "I told you everything I remember. What is it you're trying to figure out anyway? *I'd* like to know why the demon seemed interested in me. It was— It was not the most comfortable feeling I've ever had. Maybe if we brought in some of the enforcers who were nearby, they'd have some insight. I didn't get the chance to talk to any of them before we all scattered for our cars to get out of there."

The officials exchanged a glance, and that said everything. They knew something they weren't telling her. They were trying to lead her in some direction without giving her all the information, like she was on some sort of trial. Did they really think they could get away with treating the woman who'd laid so much on the line for them like a criminal?

"We'll speak with them later," Lady Northcott started in a flat voice. "Right now we'd just like to know—"

I slammed my hands into the tabletop. At the bang my palms smacking the varnished wood, everyone jumped, even Rose. The Northcotts stared at me.

"No," I said in my most menacing tone. "You've badgered Rose enough. What the hell is it that you know that you're not sharing? Cough it up! Or we're walking right out of here now. We didn't have to come help you mop up the problem *you* made, you know."

I looped my arm around Rose's. "Damon," she murmured, slightly chiding, but she reached to take my hand at the same time.

Lady Northcott's jaw worked. "I don't think it's your place to make those sorts of determinations."

Rose drew herself up straighter. "Of course it's his place—just as much as it's your consort's place to stand beside you as the head of the whole Assembly. And Damon is right. You're talking to me completely differently from before. You asked me to come here and help based on the things I'd seen. Why are you suddenly acting like *I'm* one of the traitors?"

More glances around the table. All right, I was done with this bunch. I tugged Rose. "Come on, angel. Let them come find us when they've pulled their heads out of their asses."

The second we took a step toward the door, Lady Northcott raised her hand. "No. Wait. I'm sorry. It's just... It's been difficult to wrap our heads around this."

"Around *what*?" Kyler said.

She made a dismissive gesture to the enforcers, and they slipped out of the room. "We can't be sure—" Brimsey started at the far end of the table, but Lady Northcott shook her head.

"I've seen no indication that there's any conscious affinity. She deserves to know."

"I deserve to know what?" Rose asked. Her fingers tensed around mine.

Lady Northcott sighed. "One of the enforcers who was with you during your interviews yesterday was bothered by something your father said during your interview, about our success against the demon depending on you. She asked permission to speak to him again this morning. That interrogation was conducted under truth compulsion while you were on your way to the confrontation."

"And?" Rose said when the older woman hesitated. "My father's been trying to guilt me into thinking the way he tried to bind me into a toxic consorting was necessary, not a crime. As if I'm any different from the other witches the Frankfords' faction has wrung dry."

"Oh, but you are," Lady Northcott said. A shiver ran under my skin at her tone. "You're one of the most powerful witches I've seen in my lifetime, Lady Hallowell. When I consider how little time you've had to hone your newly emerged abilities, probably *the* most powerful."

"I come from two strong magical families," Rose said.

"You do. But it's more than that." Lady Northcott hesitated, and then pushed on. "Your father shaped you for this sort of greatness from your very beginnings. You were conceived under the influence of that demonic magic."

CHAPTER NINE

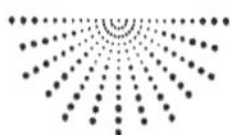

Rose

*Y*our father shaped you from your very beginnings. Even hours later, Lady Northcott's words rang in my head. Wandering around the bedroom of the hotel suite the Northcotts had set me and my consorts up in wasn't helping me escape. Everything around me was a reminder of the fears I'd provoked in the Assembly officials. They hadn't felt safe letting me stay in the building with them anymore.

I forced myself to come to a stop on the hardwood floor and dragged in a breath of the lightly freesia-scented air. The tap of Kyler's fingers against his tablet carried from the suite's living area. After my initial shock had worn off with the comfort of my consorts around me, I'd encouraged him to go back to his research. He was looking for any records that might relate to the circumstances of my conception and birth. Gabriel had gone to join him with one of the laptops we'd borrowed.

I should be out there too, searching for more information that might help, doing *something* to combat the demon's threat. But my legs balked at the thought. What if I'd already hindered our progress there more than I'd helped?

My father had told his interrogator everything. He'd had to, once they knew the right questions to ask. He'd had demonic power in him when he'd gone to my mother the night I was conceived. He'd planned the timing; he'd sent that unnatural magic into her womb to encourage a child to grow—a child who'd have even more capacity for magic than any witch should. He'd kept encouraging it, with little boosts of power as he touched my mother's growing belly, until just a few weeks before I emerged into the world.

Apparently he'd said he'd done it to free witching kind from the influence of the demons. He'd hoped that a witch with the enhancement of demonic strength would be able to seal the portal and prevent the Frankfords from ever reopening it. Maybe he'd told himself that was why he was doing it at the time, to get around any guilt he should have felt. I wasn't sure I could believe he'd ever meant to attempt that plan once he realized how much he could enjoy the extra power himself.

Even if he *had* meant to go through with it, he'd planned to enslave me to a consort who didn't give a shit about me and then force me into following his scheme, rather than telling me the truth and asking for my help like a halfway decent human being.

"Rose," Seth said softly where he was sitting at the edge of the king-sized bed. He held out his hand to me. "Do you need to talk some more? Or just sit with me. You know you're not in this alone."

A pang ran through my chest, all the love I felt for him tangled with my horror at what I'd discovered. At what I'd allowed him and the other guys to bind themselves to. But it wasn't as if I could hide my distress from him. I sat down next to him and leaned my head on his shoulder, as much for him as for me. His arm came around my waist.

"Maybe it would have worked," I said. "What we tried this morning. Maybe if I hadn't been there, if the demon hadn't sensed that I had some kind of connection to it... Maybe the magic I sent into the mix actually worked against our purpose, since I didn't know my spark might be tainted."

"The demonic power from those two guys who went with you helped you push the demon back," Jin pointed out from the armchair he'd settled into. "Any of that influence in you probably helped too. Maybe in this one case, it's not a taint, it's a bonus."

"And there can't be that much in you," Damon said, stopping in the middle of his own restless pacing to fix his gaze on me. "I know what that monster feels like, being close to it. I've never gotten even the slightest hint of that feeling from you."

"That just means the influence is buried deep. Or so merged with my spark it wouldn't show unless I tried to bring it out." I bit my lip. There was something in me, something twisted, strong enough that the demon had noticed from thirty feet away.

"It came at me, but it didn't hurt *me*," I said in a thin voice. "As if it saw me as an ally, not an enemy."

"It doesn't matter what it thinks," Damon said. "*You* know you're going to take it down. Fuck it and the whole Assembly."

Seth gave him a chiding look and nestled me closer against his brawny body. "You know now," he said. "You didn't realize before, but now you can use that power to your advantage. Turn it against the demon. You won't run out of magic the way the men who stole some of that power will."

"If the Assembly decides to trust me enough to let me get involved again at all," I said. "If the influence I've grown up with even works that way. Those men were regular people who took a little of that energy into themselves. I was *made* with it. I…"

I was a monster too, wasn't I? Some element of that creature that made my stomach turn and my nerves shiver ran through every particle of my being. I restrained a shudder now.

"You," Seth said, soft but firm, "are still exactly the same woman I fell in love with. Nothing we found out today changes that."

I looked up at him, needing to see the honesty of that statement gleaming in his gray-green eyes. He traced his fingers along my jaw and kissed me.

There was no reluctance, no hesitation in that kiss. His mouth met mine with all the hunger and affection he'd always shown me. It was a relief to lose myself in that heat, in the trickle of desire that turned into a flood as his tongue teased past the seam of my lips and his muscular chest brushed my breasts.

Damon was never one to be left out. As I fell deeper into Seth's kiss, the mattress shifted at my other side. Damon's hand came to rest on my waist, his lips brushing my bare shoulder.

"Whatever your asshole father did back then, you made yourself the woman you are," he murmured. "I couldn't want you more, exactly like this. All that crap doesn't make a bit of difference."

Jin settled onto the bed behind us. He eased my hair to the side with a gentle graze of his fingertips and kissed the most sensitive spot on the back of my neck. "You're my Briar Rose," he said. "Now and always. We've known you longer than anyone here, we've always trusted you, and do you see any of us second-guessing that now? No. And I'm more than happy to remind you just how much good we are together."

Pleasure radiated through me with every caress. Seth tugged down the zipper of my dress, and I arched into him as he slid the silky fabric down. Damon made quick work of my bra. I yanked at Seth's shirt, wanting to be even more swept away by the force of their desire, but my fingers twitched as I reached for his naked chest. The image rose up in my head of the faction member who'd demonstrated how he'd conducted the demonic power through his palm with a motion of his hand. My own palm tingled uneasily.

I'd never hurt my consorts with my touch before. But a cold thread of doubt coiled through my thoughts no matter how I tried to focus on their attentions and bringing them the same pleasure.

What if something deeper had awakened in me after this morning's encounter with the demon? What if that confrontation had jarred something loose that I hadn't needed to worry about before? I hadn't felt any different other than unsettled by its interest, but... I couldn't shake my fear.

My hand trembled against Seth's abs, my fingers curling before they found the waist of his jeans. He paused, drawing back, and the other guys hesitated in turn.

"Rose?" Seth said. "What's wrong? If you don't want this—"

"I do," I said quickly. "I do, so much. I just..." I looked down at my hands, palms up. "I don't know how much I can trust myself. I can't get that worry out of my head."

Seth frowned, but then an almost wicked glint lit in his eyes. A husky note came into his voice. "What if we took away the worry?"

"What do you mean?" I asked, heat pooling between my legs in anticipation of his answer.

Instead of speaking, he urged me farther up the bed to the plump pillows. Desire darkened Damon's expression as he followed us. A grin curved Jin's lips.

Seth undid his belt and slid it from his jeans. Ever-so-carefully, he looped it around one of my wrists and slid the buckle down so the leather band held me loosely. He touched the headboard and raised an eyebrow at me in question.

Eagerness rushed through me. To give in completely

—to put myself in their hands, figuratively and literally, with my own taken out of the equation. Yes.

I nodded, a flush creeping up my neck. Damon leaned in to kiss my collarbone as Seth tied the other end of his belt to the headboard. Then my rebel was stripping off his own belt, tossing his jeans aside for good measure. Damon slid the loop over my other wrist as tenderly as Seth had.

My fingers closed around the warm leather. I could tell, if I'd needed to yank myself free, I could have. But I didn't want to.

As Jin peeled my dress the rest of the way down my legs, Damon captured my mouth. Seth cupped one of my breasts and slicked his tongue over the already pebbled nipple. A gasp escaped me.

Every touch was heightened when I left myself to their mercy. All they wanted from me was to take whatever they hungered to give me. And by the Spark, I was hungry too.

Jin kissed his way back up to the inside of my thigh. His breath spilled hot over my core. He lowered his mouth to me, swiveling his tongue around my clit, and I moaned into Damon's mouth. My hips bucked up in encouragement I couldn't express with my hands.

"You taste perfect," my artist murmured. His fingers tested my folds and eased inside me. One and then two hooked up to reach that perfect point of pleasure as he mouthed my clit.

A giddy wave of bliss rolled over me. Seth stroked my other breast as he teased my nipple with his teeth, and Damon trailed his lips across my cheek to nip my earlobe, and for a moment nothing existed but that whirl of pleasure.

"What do you want?" Damon murmured. "Let us give it to you, angel."

A shaky breath spilled out of me. "More. Faster. I'm almost—"

Jin sped up his pumping before I'd even finished speaking, suckling me with greater intensity, and ecstasy spiked through my veins. My hips rocked into his touch, and a second later that bliss burst through me, leaving me clenching around his fingers and crying out. Seth groaned at the sight and kissed me again, hard.

"I want you inside me," I said, breathless with the need still pulsing through me. "Please."

My stalwart guardian was already stripping off his pants. Jin moved around him to claim a kiss as Seth bent over me. Seth trailed his fingertips over my folds, slick with my release. I spread my thighs as I whimpered.

He palmed his thick cock, teasing the head over my clit and down, and my head bowed back into the pillow. My grip on the belts tightened. Jin kissed his way down my neck and Damon was fondling my breasts and, oh, Seth surged into me as if he couldn't wait for us to be made one. The heady burn of the penetration spread through my whole body.

Seth tucked one arm under my hips, angling me to meet him even more closely. A moan slipped from my mouth as he filled me deeper and deeper again with each thrust. Pleasure trembled through my limbs, but it wasn't enough.

"Damon," I said around a gasp. "I want you too." I

turned my head toward him, my gaze going to the bulge of his erection through his boxers.

"Fuck," he muttered. He kicked the last of his clothes off and knelt by the pillow, just close enough that I could swipe my tongue across the head of his cock. He groaned.

"If it's too much, just pull back," he said in a rasp. He guided his length past my lips, the musky salty flavor of him filling my mouth. His fingers tangled in my hair. He started to pump his hips with gentle strokes, his breath stuttering.

My spark danced in my chest in time with the rhythm of Seth's cock driving into me, the rocking of Damon fucking my mouth. Every part of me was flooded with heat. Jin twisted my nipple, a jolt of near-pain amid the pleasure, and I soared even higher. Right then, in that embrace with three of the guys I'd have given my life for, I didn't have the slightest doubt about who I was or what I was capable of.

Seth bucked into me faster, his thumb flicking over my clit. Another wave of bliss coursed through me, building higher. My lips closed tighter around Damon's cock, and he swore with a hiss through his teeth. He gripped my hair as his hips jerked, a creamy spurt hitting the back of my mouth.

"Oh, angel." He slumped down next to me, kissing my cheek, stroking my neck. "What do you need? I want to see you come all over again."

All I needed was those words in that wanting voice. Seth drove into me one more time, and the wave crashed over me. Light crackled behind my eyes as my second orgasm sent me flying. Seth hunched over me with a few last frantic thrusts, following me and filling me with even more heat.

Damon tugged my wrist free from his belt and pressed a kiss to my palm. My heart fluttered as I drew him to me, hugging him close. Jin released my other hand and settled into my embrace on the other side, my fingers coming to rest against the smooth skin of his back. With a contented sound, Seth rested his head on my belly.

Sudden tears pricked at the back of my eyes, but they were mostly happy. I trusted my guys—and they trusted me. Why should I doubt that trust? Jin was right: They knew me better than any person in the Assembly did.

I couldn't be certain how much of the demon's influence I carried inside me, but I'd be damned if I let an enemy lurking within destroy everything I'd fought so hard for.

CHAPTER TEN

Rose

"I don't get it," Naomi said through the phone. "Why did they drag you all the way out there just to tell you to back off?"

I sank into the pillows on the hotel bed, rubbing my forehead. I'd wanted to talk to my cousin, mainly to find out how things were going back on my estate, but I still hadn't figured out how much and how soon to tell her about the past day's revelations. All I'd vented about so far was the fact that the Northcotts had asked me to step back from their strategy meetings.

"There's just been stuff that's come up," I improvised. "With my dad, and my childhood—he raised me to be demon chow, basically, right? They hadn't thought through all the implications."

"Well, I still think that's a ridiculous reason to shut you out. You're the one who got to the bottom of this whole scandal in the first place, and you and your consorts risked your lives to do that while they sat there oblivious. They should be kissing your feet in gratitude that you're still helping them at all."

I had to laugh a little at her no-nonsense tone, so very Naomi, even though my stomach was still knotted tight. A couple months ago, I hadn't known I *had* a cousin, but she'd staked out a spot in my life with immediate spirited determination I couldn't help appreciating.

"I wish you were here," I said, frowning at the molded ceiling.

"Well... You might get your wish very soon."

The sly note in her voice made me sit up. I knit my brow. "What do you mean? You aren't thinking of—"

The roar of a gunning engine carried through the phone line. My eyes widened. "Naomi, where are you?"

"I, ah, might be in a car just making our way through Portland right now," Naomi said. "Surprise!"

For a second, I was speechless. Then my mind latched on to one part of her comment. "*We?*" She obviously wasn't the one driving.

"Lesley wanted to come along—and who can blame her. I didn't want to leave her on the estate with no company. And my mom flew in after she heard. And, ah, so did Aunt Irene."

My back tensed. Aunt Irene, older sister to my late mother and to Naomi's mother, my aunt Ginny, had almost definitely tipped the Assembly off to some of our plans back when we'd been labeled as criminals and in the enforcers' sights. She might not have known me well, but she'd betrayed me just to make sure she stayed out of the line of fire. I could only imagine what she'd think of this latest discovery if she found out.

"What's *she* doing here?" I said. "What are either of them doing here? The Assembly has been trying to keep a close lid on— You didn't tell them the whole story, did you?"

"Not exactly," Naomi said. "Do you really think the Assembly could hide something this big for very long, after all the arrests, and with all the enforcer movements on the coast? Everyone's buzzing about *something* going on. I told Mom a little, hoping she'd worry less, and, well, it kind of backfired."

"You'd better believe it did!" Aunt Ginny's voice carried faintly from somewhere near Naomi.

"Okay," I said. "Okay." My pulse was skittering. They were coming here. I was going to have to explain everything else somehow. I could already tell if they didn't understand the Assembly's decision to shunt me over here out of the way, they'd probably march right over there in protest, and then they'd hear about my demon-tainted magic from someone like Lady Northcott. At least if they got the story from me, I'd know they had my side.

My fingers gripped the phone tighter, and Naomi let out a pleased exclamation. "There's the Assembly building now! You want to come meet us out front, cuz? I don't know if the security people are going to be super happy with us marching right in."

"Oh," I said, my heart jumping. I had to explain things *now*. "Er. I'm not actually at the Assembly building anymore. They ended up moving us to a hotel down the street... It's a long story."

"What?" Naomi said. "I guess we'd better hear that long story when we do get to you."

Despite my dread, I gave her the directions to the hotel. With her promise that they'd be here in five minutes, I hung up the phone. My throat had constricted.

I'd only just reconnected with my mom's family. They were the only family I'd been able to trust after what Dad had put me through. Was I going to lose them too now, as soon as I told them the truth?

Out in the suite's living room, Kyler was peering intently at his laptop screen—surprise, surprise. Jin was sketching something on a pad of paper, and Damon had passed out for a nap on the couch across from him. Gabriel turned where he was pouring himself a cup of coffee in the kitchenette area. Seth had gone out about an hour ago to check about supplies for a plan he'd been working out— one he hadn't wanted to even tell me much about until he was sure he could get the materials he needed.

One the Assembly might not even bother to try, the way things were going.

"How are things back home?" Gabriel asked.

"I don't know," I said. "Naomi's on her way *here*, with my aunts and Lesley. I have to go down and meet them in the lobby."

He set down his mug, his expression showing he'd already guessed my fears. "I'll come with you."

"It's okay, really. I—"

"Rose. I'll come with you."

Jin got up. "I wouldn't mind stretching my legs too."

Ky looked around at us, his eyes a little dazed from all that time staring at screens. "You don't need me, right? I think I might have found something that'll help with Seth's idea..." He made a grabbing motion toward Gabriel with a smile. "Pass me that coffee if you're not going to drink it?"

Gabriel chuckled and set the mug on the desk beside Ky as he made his way to meet me at the door. I looked down at myself, at the dress that was a little wrinkled from my hasty packing when the Assembly had summoned us. Oh, it wasn't as if my family was going to decide how they felt about my situation based on the neatness of my clothing.

The three of us headed down on the elevator. Jin rubbed my back soothingly, and Gabriel squeezed my hand. "Nothing has really changed, Sprout," he said. "They'll see that."

I swallowed hard. "I hope so."

We reached the lobby just as Naomi and the others were coming through the front doors. "Rose!" Naomi cried, and hustled over to give me a hug. Lesley trailed behind her shyly, and my aunts headed for the lobby desk. Ginny shot me a warm smile. Irene gave me an unreadable look.

I hugged my cousin back, choking up just to have her here. "We managed to book a couple rooms over the phone on the way over," Naomi said as she pulled back. "Fastest travel arrangements ever!" She grinned. "When they let us in, we'll lug our suitcases up there, and then I need to hear the full story about why the Assembly people are being such asses. Hey, Gabriel, Jin!" She offered my consorts a little wave.

I wasn't sure if it'd have felt better to spill this secret right there in the lobby, versus having to hold it in the whole way back up to the floor they were staying on, but I couldn't start talking about magic and demons in front of all the hotel's unsparked clientele. After dropping off their suitcases, my aunts came with the rest of us into the room Naomi and Lesley were sharing. Naomi dropped down onto the edge of one of the beds and motioned for me to sit in the armchair near the TV.

"All right," she said with a swish of her chestnut ponytail. "Let's hear it. I want to know who to direct my righteous fury at."

I tried to smile, but my control over my mouth wavered. Gabriel and Jin came up to flank me, Gabriel resting a hand on my shoulder. I could have asked them to do the explaining, but that didn't feel right.

"I guess if you're going to direct fury at anyone," I said, "it should probably be my dad. There was more than we knew going on after he and my mom got married. He—" I paused to collect myself, glancing at my aunts. "Naomi told you about the Frankfords, and the demons, and how they were using the witches?"

Aunt Ginny's expression darkened. "We got the gist of it. Bastards."

Her anger bolstered my courage, but only a little. "Well, in case you didn't know about this part, the whole arrangement with the demons, it was so the men in that faction could take some of the power from that plane of existence into themselves. So that they could use it, like we use our spark, to change things. It doesn't last the same way, so they had to keep going back. But that's not the point. The point is— When my parents were trying to get pregnant— I don't really know why he did it—"

My voice caught in my throat, trying to get to the heart of the matter. The choked-up feeling I'd had before overwhelmed me. My eyes went hot. Before I could catch them, tears started leaking out.

"Rose!" Aunt Ginny said, sounding so concerned her voice only made me sob.

I pressed my hand to my mouth, fighting for composure. Jin knelt next to me, threading his arm around mine. Gabriel squeezed my shoulder. They were here with me. No matter what happened with my mother's family, I wasn't alone.

Aunt Ginny was here with me too. She crouched down in front of me, taking my free hand in hers. "You don't have to talk about it," she said gently. "Not now. Not ever if you don't want to. It's all right."

A laugh sputtered out of me. "No, it's not. And you'll find out anyway if I don't. So..." I dragged in a breath and forced myself to start telling the revised account of my conception.

Ginny stayed where she was as my explanation came out, the others frozen where they were poised on the two beds, Naomi's eyes growing wider by the minute. By the time I finished, my body was trembling. I gritted my teeth and willed myself steady.

"So, that's why I'm here and not with the Assembly," I said. "That power must have affected me. I've got some kind of connection to the demons, including the one they're trying to push back. They don't want it using me or me helping it somehow. I guess that makes sense."

I looked up cautiously. Naomi pushed herself to her feet, her jaw set and her eyes narrowed.

"It doesn't," she snapped. "It doesn't make any sense at all. If you *do* have that connection, which obviously doesn't endear those monsters to you anyway, you might be the key to figuring this whole mess out."

Her words echoed my father's comment the other day. My gut twisted, but hearing that sentiment coming from her didn't hold the same pressure. From my cousin, it was a statement that she believed in me.

Aunt Ginny was shaking her head. "I can't imagine— If we'd had any idea he was going to those lengths— Oh, Spark help us, poor Alora. Poor *you*." She tugged on my hand, and I let her pull me into her arms. Like the mother I should have had, I thought, and almost started bawling all over again.

They were horrified, but for me, not by me.

At least, some of them were. My gaze found Aunt Irene, sitting stiffly on the bed. When our eyes met, I was surprised to see hers were watery.

She lowered her head. "Virginia's right," she said, sounding weary. "We should have done more."

"You didn't know," I said quietly. "*I* didn't even know until yesterday. I doubt Mom had much of any idea."

"Yes, but—" She grimaced and met my gaze again. "I'm sorry. You've been a stranger to me, one I assumed followed your father's path since he was the one who raised you. I let my anger with him and my fears for my family determine my actions. You didn't deserve that. You're a victim of his schemes just as much as my little sister ever was. I should have defended you as much as I would have her."

I stared at her, not sure what to say. I'd never expected an apology. Did I even believe it?

Did it matter? She wasn't condemning me. I wasn't going to trust her any time soon, but I didn't have to shun her if she wasn't shunning me.

"Well, now what?" Naomi said. "There's a demon on the loose and the Assembly is acting like a bunch of idiots. We didn't come all this way just to sit around."

Aunt Ginny stood up, resolve hardening her expression. "We go to the Assembly right now and bring every bit of influence *we* have as the Levesques. And we do have some, even if we aren't in the Portland crowd. We know enough to make life very difficult for the Northcotts and their associates if we wanted to."

I looked up at her, my spirits lifting. "You think that'll work?"

She smiled tightly. "Nothing gained without trying. But yes. You can't do better than a united front. Come on. Let's set them straight before they bungle this catastrophe any more than they already have."

CHAPTER ELEVEN

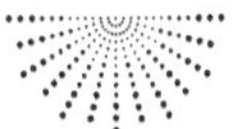

Seth

The smell of soldered metal filled the air in the abandoned parking lot the Assembly had given over to our use. Somewhere behind me, tools were hissing and bars clanking against each other. I wiped the sweat off my forehead and inspected the massive wall of twisted copper and steel that was standing mostly upright in front of me.

The steel sections were just there to bolster the softer metal. Kyler had found a reference to the demons' dislike to copper in the Frankfords' records, so I'd wanted to incorporate as much as possible into the structure. We were fixing the bars in the shapes of glyphs intended to strengthen the walls and to contain and subdue whatever lay inside them.

If this plan worked, the demon on the loose would be caged by tomorrow.

Jin came up beside me. After all the work he'd done incorporating glyphs into paintings for practical use—and he had done some metal work for sculptures in the past too—I'd appreciated having him consult on the designs. He looked the wall over, cocking his head.

"If you don't think it'd hurt the structural integrity or whatever to add them, we could work in a few more of the binding glyphs," he said, pointing. "Fit them around this corner here, and the curve in the shielding one there."

With the movement of his finger, I could picture it. I nodded. "Good thinking. I'll add those in right away."

Right away wasn't all that fast when I was doing this right. I sketched out the addition to be sure of it and worked the metal into shape slowly and methodically. Soldering it into the existing structure required the most care. I didn't want to jar any of the seams that were already secured.

When I'd finished that enhancement, I ambled across the lot to check on the handful of workers the Assembly had brought in to help get this project done. The basic framework for the other five sections of the cage was in place and the larger details coming together well. I made a couple of suggestions—"Add a little more steel here." "Make sure you support that bend."—but mostly all I needed to offer was praise. I'd put a lot of time into the plans I'd written up to make sure every aspect was covered before we even got started.

I checked my phone. It was mid-afternoon now. I still had to take care of the more intricate glyphs on three of the walls. We'd better be ready to cage that demon tomorrow. The main—and maybe the only—reason the Assembly had approved this plan and Rose's involvement was that since the confrontation a couple of days ago, the creature had picked up its speed. And its ferocity. In the last two days, it had killed a dozen people who'd crossed its path.

If we didn't stop it soon, it'd reach way more inhabited areas. The thought of what might happen then made me wince inwardly. We'd just been lucky so far that the towns near it now were few and far between.

I'd just fixed a few more strips of copper onto what would become the cage's floor and was reaching for another when the gleam of familiar black hair caught my eye. Rose came up on the other side of the work table that held my tools, her cousin and two of the other young witches in tow.

"Jin said at least a couple of the walls are ready for us to get to work doing the magicking for them?" she said.

The plan was for the witches to spread out the work —some enforcers were due to show up to lend a hand too —but Rose needed to add her touch to every spell. We were hoping that imbuing each glyph with a little demon-influenced power would make them more effective than the past spells the enforcers had tried.

"That one's finished," I said, pointing to the wall I'd added the final elements to earlier. "And this one almost is."

"Wow," Naomi said, taking in the propped up metal square I was working on. It was more than twice as tall as I was and equally wide. I'd been standing on a step ladder a lot of the time. "So how is this all going to come together? Is there some kind of bait we can use, like a mouse trap?"

Rose shook her head. "We don't want the demon to realize it's a cage at all," she said. "Seth has it figured out so we can have all the sections spread out, with a base we can easily attach to a truck once we're ready. We know we could move the demon a little in a direction we wanted before. We shove it onto the base, and then we push the walls and ceiling up around it magically."

"There'll be glyphs on the locking mechanisms too," I said. "That thing is going to be completely surrounded by magic."

Caroline, the posh-looking young woman whose blouse and dress pants looked pretty out of place in this construction yard, clapped her hands. "Well, let's get to work on that spell-casting, then. The more magic we can pour into these walls, the better they'll hold."

"That's the idea," Rose said. She wet her lips. "And there's the other aspect too..."

Lesley, the reserved witch who'd lived with us on Rose's estate for a few weeks, tucked her mousy brown hair behind her ears. "We're adding blood to the mix," she said in a soft even voice. "We know. We all agreed to that part too."

"I just—I wouldn't blame you if it seemed a bit too much now that we're faced with actually doing it." Rose gave a nervous laugh. "The Northcotts wanted the bloodletting to only happen with enforcer supervision, so I guess we don't have to worry about it just yet."

"From what we've heard from the witches the Frankfords' faction used and from their records, it could make a big difference," I said. From what my brother had said, the faction members hadn't been completely clear on how the whole bodily sacrifice thing worked. But it had seemed as if sacrifices made with the intention of pushing them back worked more powerfully than any magic on its own.

But when it came to blood spilled not in purposeful sacrifice but random violence, it seemed the demons could use it to their own purposes. That death at the Cliff, the Frankford guard fallen onto the rocks, had *given* them power. A thought that made me even more unsettled by the idea of the demon reaching an actual town. How much more powerful would it get if it was murdering hundreds or thousands instead of a handful of people each day?

Rose leaned in to give me a peck on the cheek before moving with the others to the finished wall. I threw myself back into my own job. I noticed distantly when a couple squads of enforcers showed up a half hour later to lend their own magical energy to the cause, but for the most part I wasn't paying attention to anything except the pieces of metal in front of me. That was the closest thing to magic I knew how to work.

A pink tint was creeping across the horizon with the coming evening when I straightened up from the structure that would form the cage's roof. I had one more wall to put the final touches on, and we'd need to test out the hinges before we sent everything off with the truck tomorrow, but we were almost there. A prickling burn spread through my muscles as I stretched my arms up and then in front of me.

Rose was leaning against one of the cars, her cheeks wan. Frowning, I went to join her.

"Is everything all right?" I asked. I'd been so lost in the metalworking I'd barely talked to her since she'd arrived—but then, she'd seemed busy with the magic-working every time I'd looked her way. Rose was every bit as dedicated to getting this done as I was.

She nodded and gave me a tight smile. "Just taking a bit of a breather."

"You're not straining your spark, are you, putting so much magic into this?" In spite of how tired I was too, a quiver of lust shot to my groin at the thought of the ways we could stoke that flame.

My consort squeezed my arm reassuringly. "No, I've got plenty of energy to draw on. It's just that drawing out the demonic aspect within it..." She looked at the ground, her voice lowering too. "I can feel it, when I delve deeply enough, now that I know to look for it. There's a hint of that impression I get when I'm near the demons, like a faint aftertaste—but I can condense it if I try hard enough. But doing that takes more out of me than regular magicking."

I wrapped my arms around her and tugged her to me, taking her weight for as long as she'd let me. "If this works, you shouldn't ever have to draw on it again."

"That's what I keep telling myself." She nestled her head against my chest for just a few seconds, and then she eased back with a sigh. "I should get back to it. We've got a couple more to finish."

I let her go with a pang in my chest. After everything she'd done to escape her father, his machinations had tied her to the demons anyway. Maybe we should be grateful that her powers might be the answer to stopping this menace... but no one person should have that much responsibility on her shoulders. If I could have taken more of the burden from her, I would have.

As I headed over to the last section that needed detailing, a new car pulled into the lot. Mr. Northcott stepped out with a couple of enforcers. His tall form looked tense as he scanned the yard. His pale eyes came to rest on me. He headed over with brisk strides, running a hand through his gray hair.

"Mr. Lennox," the co-head of the Witching Assembly said, taking in the wall I'd been about to work on. "Since the day is almost over, I was hoping to get an in-person progress report. Where are we at?"

"We should have the last wall fully constructed by early tomorrow morning at the latest," I said. "And then of course the final spells will need to be added, and there'll be some testing to conduct. I can't see any reason we shouldn't be ready to put the plan into action by the afternoon, though."

Northcott's lips pursed. "There's no way you could speed along that process? We want to get this cage out there and in action as early as we can."

The guy had only been on the lot for five minutes, and already he was trying to call the shots. "If you want it done right, we need to take the time to make sure everything will work the way we want," I said. "And the witches doing the casting will need rest to recover overnight, won't they?"

His mouth stayed tight, but he couldn't deny that.

"Just see it's done as quickly as you can manage," he said. "The demon claimed two more victims an hour ago. The longer that menace is on the loose..."

"I know," I said, a little sharply than was maybe completely polite. But the Assembly officials had managed to miss the conspiracy under their noses, all the women who'd been hurt by the faction and their demons, for so long before now. Decades upon decades. It was a little much for him to complain about the difference of a few hours.

Mr. Northcott gave me a measured look. "My consort and I don't take our leadership of the witching community lightly, young man. Every death that happens due to the actions of those under our rule— every death that comes *to* those under our rule—we must shoulder. We couldn't have imagined facing a catastrophe like this when we were striving for the position we hold, you know."

No, I guessed they couldn't have. "We're working as hard as we can," I said, less brusquely. "As soon as it's ready, you'll hear about it."

"Good." He nodded briskly and strode off to survey the rest of the lot's activity. My jaw clenched as I turned back to the wall.

Maybe I *could* finish this tonight. If it made the difference between a few more people dying...

I grabbed the next copper piece and my welding torch. My fingers clamped around the warm metal. Fix it into place with the solder. Meld and bend it with the heat. Just like that. Just a little—

I caught my hand a split-second before I twisted the

piece too far. I'd nearly damaged the glyph already in place above it. Lowering the torch, I took a deep breath in and out.

There's no place for panic on the site. My dad used to say that when he was teaching me the ropes of the reno and construction business. It applied here too, maybe even more than there.

I reached out with steadier hands and picked up the next piece at my usual pace. Steady and careful had always gotten me where I needed to be in the past. I had to trust it would again.

Rose

The fabric of the new T-shirt and sweats hung a little stiffly on my body. I supposed they'd need a few washes to break in, but I didn't have time for that. I was supposed to be joining the enforcers in our second effort to send the demon back to whence it came in a little more than an hour. If sweats worked for the closest thing the Assembly had to an army, then I'd figured I might as well give them a try. Maximum flexibility of movement couldn't be a bad thing when casting the most important spells of my life.

I tugged at the light cotton as I came back into the hotel suite's living room. All the guys except for Kyler had come with Seth and me to help with the final physical testing of Seth's cage, and I'd returned a little early to prepare for my next part in that plan. Ky, for once in the last few days, was away from his computer and the desk, fishing a couple slices of pizza out of the delivery box from last night's hasty dinner.

A wave of fondness washed over me as I ambled over to him in the kitchenette. When he'd closed the fridge, I nudged him with my elbow. "I was starting to think you'd permanently bonded with that laptop. Are you going to give yourself more than a five-second break, or are you taking your lunch back to work?"

Ky grinned at me, but his expression looked a little weary. I wasn't sure how much sleep he'd been letting himself get. "Pizza makes an excellent side dish to data-diving."

A sharper emotion pierced through my heart. I caught his hand before he could pick up the plate, peering into his normally cheerful eyes. Even their usual light had dimmed a bit.

"Since we moved to the hotel, you've been poring over those records even more than before," I said. "I know, we've all been busy, but..." But I'd still had moments of closeness with all my other consorts since then. I swallowed hard. "If it bothers you—what we found out about what I am, what's influencing my magic —and you need some space from that, I'd get it. I just want to know."

Kyler's eyebrows jumped up. He didn't speak but simply cupped my face with both hands and pulled my mouth to his. His kiss was so tender and yet determined that my worries melted away.

When he eased back, he kept his head bowed close enough that I felt his breath on my cheek. "It's not that, Rose. It's nothing like that at all, and I'm sorry if I gave you that impression. Finding that out, seeing how finding it out upset *you*, I wanted to dig up any answers that could help you as quickly as I can. Between that and what we've heard about the demon's behavior... I guess I haven't given myself room to think about anything else."

A different sort of lump filled my throat. I kissed him again, quick but hard. "I'm sorry for fretting. I shouldn't have even thought—I must be letting the shock get to me too much."

"Learning something like that has got to be a lot to take in," Ky said. "And you haven't exactly had much downtime to make your peace with the idea." He stroked his fingers down my cheek, gazing at me intently. "If you need me *here*, with you, not on the computer, you just need to say so. Is something else bothering you?"

"Other than the usual?" I said with a short laugh. But maybe there was something. I rubbed my mouth. "I'm doing another circle with the faction's witches before I leave. Or at least that's what we had planned. If I'm going to help them with their recovery, I think they need to know the whole truth about who they're dealing with."

"You had nothing to do with the Frankfords," Ky said. "You never purposefully had anything to do with the demons."

I gave him a crooked smile. "They're traumatized, for good reason. If anything about me reminds them of the horrible experiences they went through—or could remind them—I wouldn't blame them for wanting to avoid me. They should get to make that choice. Their consorts and families took enough other choices away from them already."

"Fair enough." He waggled a slice of pizza. "Pepperoni and olives to fortify you for the day?"

"I had something in the car on the way back," I said. A roast beef sandwich that was now sitting heavy in the bottom of my stomach. "You need your fortifications too."

"Not half as much as you do." His hand slid to my waist as I started to move away. He held me there for a second longer. "You're heading out for the big mission right after your 'circle,' right?"

I nodded. "They were just putting the last touches on the cage when I left."

Ky's face turned serious again. "Look after yourself, all right? I know everyone's got all these expectations, but it *isn't* all on you to fix this."

"I know." I touched his face. "I promise, there's nothing I want more than to be back here with you as soon as humanly possible."

He leaned in to kiss me again, and I wished I could just lose myself in the heat of his mouth, the strength of his lanky body. But I had people waiting for me.

When I made it down to the lobby, Naomi was waiting for me. "Ready?" she asked.

"Yes. Thanks for doing this."

"Of course," my cousin said as we set off down the street for the Assembly building. "Being here, helping somehow, is a hell of a lot better than wandering around your manor pretending I'm not freaking out about what might be happening. I'm ready to dive in if that's what they need."

Thalia was waiting for us in the Assembly building's front hall. I'd already talked to her about my father's recent revelations. Was her gaze a little more wary than before as she looked us over? Her smile didn't look any less warm.

"They're all gathering in the usual room," she said. "I told them you had something to discuss with them before we got started."

"Okay." I dragged in a breath. "Let's go."

This was only the third time I'd come to do our healing ritual with the recovering witches, but I could already sense a difference as I walked into the room. Most of the women stood straighter, their posture more confident than when I'd first seen them. The smiles aimed my way as we came in looked more relaxed than tight, although some of them faltered when they noticed the unfamiliar figure who'd joined us.

It'd be a while before they got their trust back completely, but they were on their way. I'd helped with that. I could take some pride in that fact even if I wasn't sure I'd get to continue those efforts.

"Thalia said there was something you needed to talk about with us?" Eloise said, her unnaturally aged face creasing even more with worry.

"It's nothing that will necessarily affect you at all," I said to her quickly. "I— Well, I suppose we'd better get everyone gathered around so I can explain the whole thing at once."

The other witches clustered around me. They stood close to each other more easily than before too, with less cringing at sharing their personal space. Another bit of progress.

I looked down at my hands, clasped tight in front of

me, and then back up at the women watching me. Crystal bobbed lightly on her heels with obvious impatience. Selena, her expression placid as ever, dipped her ivory-white head to me.

"It's meant a lot to me to be able to help you come back to your magic and your sense of security," I said. "I'd like to keep being here for you if I can. But I've recently found something out that might change the way *you* feel about me, and I didn't think it was right to keep it from you."

"Are you all right?" Crystal asked, frowning with concern.

"I think so," I said with a pang that she'd thought first of how I was doing. "I'm still me. It's just changed how I have to perceive certain aspects of myself." There was no beating around the bush. I squared my shoulders and barreled onward. "The power those witching men gained from the demons—my father took some into himself at times. And he used it to help bring me into being when he and my mother were trying to conceive. He brought more to me as I was growing inside her to encourage the growth of my potential spark..."

All around me, faces had gone rigid with horror. My chest constricted, but I forced myself to keep going.

"My spark, my magic, has been partly shaped by that power. Now that I know to look for it, I can feel hints of it within that energy, the way I draw on it, the way it moves through me." I swallowed thickly. "I thought I was a powerful witch because of my heritage. I had no idea that anything monstrous played a role. Now that I do know... After what you've all been through, I'd understand if you were uncomfortable letting your magic mingle with mine, being touched by any of that energy. I don't want to cause anyone here any more distress."

Thalia squeezed my arm steadyingly. I bobbed my head to her in thanks and motioned Naomi forward.

"This is my cousin Naomi. She hasn't experienced everything I have, but she's seen some of the chaos from the last several weeks. She'll stand by you as much as I have, if that's what you decide works best for you."

"I'd be happy to take up the role Rose has been filling in your circle," Naomi put in. "Neither of us wants you to feel you have no choice in whether to continue at all or in who you move forward with."

A murmur passed between the witches. They drew back a step, pulling closer to each other as they exchanged anxious glances. I held my hands motionless in front of me, fighting the urge to fidget.

Then Crystal moved forward. She didn't hesitate, but touched my wrist, looking me straight in the eyes. Her chin lifted.

"I've never felt anything evil in you. Nothing like those fiends. I don't feel anything evil in you now. We've all been affected by our time with the demons, but that doesn't make any of us a threat. It shouldn't make you one either."

I blinked hard. "Thank you," I said.

"Thank *you*," she said. "You trusted us to make our own decision. That's all I need to know about it."

Eloise eased forward too, and then Selena, brushing their fingers over my hands in turn like a ritual in itself. The tension in the group started to dissipate, the murmurs giving way to insistent voices. "Nothing about her magic hurt us before." "It isn't her fault."

Selena came right up beside me and patted my shoulder, her lips curved in a sad smile. "You really are one of us," she said in her soft dry voice. "Controlled and used by people you should have been able to count on in ways you couldn't understand. That only confirms that you belong here."

It hadn't entirely been a surprise that my consorts had accepted this new information about what was in me, and my family hadn't even seen the demons to fully comprehend the implications. To be embraced by these women who had so many reasons to fear me...

My heart swelled with gratitude. For the first time since Lady Northcott had delivered her announcement, I was sure that I wasn't any more broken than the unfaltering witches around me.

"Shall we go ahead with the healing circle as planned, then?" Thalia asked, and was answered by a barrage of voices insisting that we did.

I found myself in that ring of shared power again, Thalia at my right and Crystal at my left, the warmth of my spark tickling through my limbs. I took one last look around the circle before I closed my eyes to fully concentrate on the magicking. There was so much strength in this group of witches that no demon had been able to drain out of them.

I couldn't help wishing that somehow they could both have been ready to help us challenge the demon tomorrow and also never have to face one of those creatures ever again.

CHAPTER THIRTEEN

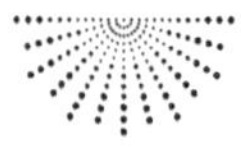

Rose

Our first drive out to challenge the demon hadn't exactly been fun and games, but the atmosphere in the jeep this afternoon felt even more somber. Naomi, Lesley, Caroline, and my aunts were all coming out to the site of the trap too, but I'd been stuck in a vehicle surrounded by enforcers. From their solemn silence and the twitchy glances they shot my way, I got the impression they thought they might have to protect themselves from me.

My skin itched with nervous anticipation. I rubbed my arms and tried to relax into the seat. Not much chance of that happening. Too much was riding on this effort. The safety of everyone the demon might hurt, the Assembly's trust in me and my consorts... My own faith in myself.

"We're pulling off up here," the enforcer in the front

said to the driver. A minute later we eased onto the grassy shoulder of the isolated road. The demon had roamed into the rolling forested land here, weaving this way and that, but keeping enough to a predictable path that the Assembly officials had been able to estimate where it would head in the next hour or so.

The enforcers stuck close by my sides as we tramped through the brush. Tangy cypress scent washed over me on the hot summer breeze. About a five-minute walk from the road, the trees opened up to a clearing of scruffy grass and wildflowers. A dilapidated cabin stood off to the side, next to an overgrown lane that was still functional enough that we'd be able to drive the truck along it to drop off the cage. Hopefully soon we'd be driving it back to collect its cargo.

The panels of the cage itself were sprawled across the floor of the clearing, one wall leaning against a couple of tree trunks where there hadn't been quite enough room to spread it out completely flat. Seth was already there, stalking around the perimeter, stopping to prod one joint and another.

My pulse hiccupped when I saw him. He must have come straight from the construction lot when they'd brought the cage out here. I'd thought he'd finish his work back there.

It was hard not to notice that a couple of the enforcers trailed behind me as I went over to him. At least they kept a bit of distance rather than lurking right at my back. I wondered which of the officials had instructed them not to let me get too far from their reach.

What had they been instructed to watch *for*, and what were they supposed to do to me if they saw that?

The sunlight in the clearing lit Seth's tawny hair with a warm glow. Despite the tension in his face, he managed to bring a lot of warmth to his smile too when he saw me approaching.

"It all looks good to go," he said. "Everything should move and latch together the way we discussed."

"We didn't discuss you being here," I said. "Seth, if this plan doesn't work, or even if the demon puts up a real fight, which it probably will…"

"I know," he said, before I had to point out that he couldn't protect himself even as well as the average witch here could. "I remembered what you said to Damon before about distractions. A few of the witching men who've been helping with the construction work came along to set things up, but they're driving back to the city in a few minutes."

Relief washed away a little of my nerves. "Good. I want you heading back with them. You've already done more than your part here."

"You know if I thought it'd help you more than distract you, I'd stay," he said.

"I do. You don't have to worry about me doubting your commitment." I poked his chest. "What I *want* is you as far away from that thing as possible."

With all the enforcers milling around, it didn't feel like the right time or place for much of a PDA. Seth grasped my arm and pressed a quick kiss to my forehead, and that would have to be enough.

"I'll be waiting for you back home," he said.

"I'll see you there," I replied, willing those words to be a promise.

Someone shouted for Seth over by the lane. I gave him a little shove, and he brushed his hand over my cheek before he loped over to join the other men. My heart ached, watching him go.

This would not be the last time I saw him. I wouldn't let it be.

"Let's go," one of the enforcers near me said. "The observers say the demon should be in range in about fifteen minutes. We need to get into position. It's a few degrees off course."

I nodded and followed her and the primary squads deeper into the woods. We had two tasks to accomplish: pushing the demon onto the right path to bring it to the clearing, and then propelling it all the way onto the cage's base so that we could close those walls around it. The first part, at least, we could be subtle about. We didn't want the fiend to know it was under assault until as late as possible.

The same sergeant who'd led our previous effort was calling out names and pointing every squad into position. I took my place on the twig-scattered ground behind the main mass of enforcers, in about the middle of the formation. I was supposed to be lending power to all of them, as much as I could. Although from the looks some of them shot over their shoulders at me, maybe they were worried I'd end up using that power on them.

A fresh prickle crept down my back. I shook it off. When we were finished here today, they'd know they could count on me.

We fell into a hush. The sergeant gave a soft call and gestured for us to move forward several paces. The demon must have adjusted its course again.

The erratic vibrations of its unearthly energy trickled over us. My back stiffened as I braced myself for that pulsing to intensify. There was a crunching, crackling sound in the distance, getting louder as the creature shambled closer to us.

The sergeant motioned for us to begin the redirection spells. Or rather, for the enforcers to begin them. As they swayed in their silent magicking, I brought my hands to my chest and spread my arms into the air, looped them around my body and unraveled them again. With every movement, I concentrated harder on the unsettling vibration I could summon from my own spark when I focused on it.

The sensation of the demonic influence in me tremored through my chest and limbs. I passed it on with the flow of my magic to the enforcers all along our line. A little of the power the demon held, to push against its inherent strange magic. It had worked when the men from the Frankford's faction had contributed their stored power. I had a nearly endless supply.

The quavering of the demon's presence rose as the sounds of its destructive arrival grew louder. Trees groaned and toppled several paces from where we stood; branches on those closer wilted when the creature paused. I reached into myself and called forth that eerie essence even faster.

Don't look this way. Don't stop. Just keep going where we tell you to.

The enforcers' spells combined with my demon-flavored magic seemed to be working. The demon shifted to one side and shuffled on toward the place where the cage was waiting. Our formation shifted in turn, all of us easing along beside the demon's path. I could barely see the creature, just a reddish glow and glimpses of knobby limbs between the trees, but my stomach was churning with the sense of its presence.

Just a little farther. As soon as the sergeant gave the signal...

At the edge of the clearing, the demon stopped. It made a grunting sort of groan low in its throat. A chill flooded me.

It could tell. It must be able to detect the magic we'd put into the cage, or maybe the copper was already repelling it.

It started to wheel, and the sergeant jerked her hand. All at once, the enforcers all around me whirled faster. I launched myself into the movements of my form with all the strength I had in me.

Our magic hummed in my ears, nearly drowning out the demon's discordant energy. We threw it toward the demon with the force of a hurricane.

My spark sputtered in my chest as I heaved my magic to join the push. An ache split down the center of me behind my ribs. I choked on a breath and kept moving, kept following the dance of casting. It would hurt a hell of a lot more if the demon turned on us.

The demon stumbled a few feet into the clearing and then reared up on its haunches. As it started to swing toward us, my heart stuttered. No. We could do this. We almost had it.

I threw myself into the magicking even faster and more furiously than I had before. My spark flared and seared all through my body. I gritted my teeth against the pain and hurled another massive force toward the demon.

Several of the enforcers' heads jerked around as my spell sang past them, their eyes wide and jaws going slack. The burst of propulsion smacked into the demon just as it twisted around. It sprawled on its back, its shoulders smacking the edge of the cage. So fucking close.

The unsettling tremor in my spark expanded, gnawing at my nerves. But as I whipped another bolt of magic toward the monster, I felt right down to the base of my teeth how my magic, with that taint, crashed right up against the demon's presence and held, not dispersing like our spells last time had. I was matching fire with fire this time.

The sergeant was hollering, and the enforcers around me were flinging out their own magic with the pattering of their feet and the darting of their hands. If we could just bring it all together—if I could send that awful flavor from my own magic across all of their castings—maybe we could win this day yet.

My foot stumbled on the uneven ground, but I caught myself and spun on. The magic wrenched through me as I tossed more and more of it out across the crowd to merge with their spells. The forest around me blurred. I sucked in air and dug down even deeper.

The demon roared, a sound that seemed to echo all the way from that other plane of its regular existence. A fresh blast of our magic hit it, and it toppled farther onto the cage. Then it shoved its massive body up and around.

I scrambled for more magic, more, more, clutching at my spark and wringing all the power I could from its dwindling flame—

My spark sputtered, and my vision hazed. A splintered pain radiated through every inch of my body. My legs sagged. As I fell to the forest floor, the last thing I saw before my sight went completely dark was the demon yanking the cage from the ground and hurling it toward the trees. Then my eyes and my mind blanked out.

* * *

"Lady Hallowell? Can you hear me?"

The tight voice penetrated the fog in my head. I blinked, my eyelids heavy as lead, and a headache pierced through my brain and down into my chest in what felt like a thousand directions. My whole body flinched.

"Hey," the woman leaning over me said, her tone softening. "There you are. Stay still. I'll do what I can to make you more comfortable."

She set her hand over my forehead and drew a glyph with a dance of her fingers. A numbing cold spread over my scalp. It dulled most, if not all, of the pain.

As the agony receded, my surroundings came into focus. I was sprawled on my back, knees raised, in a car that was bumping along some road, the rumble of its motor sounding through the padding of the seat. My head was on the witch's lap. One of the medics who'd come with us to— Oh, dear Spark.

I tried to speak, but my tongue tangled. It took a minute or two, swallowing past the dryness in my throat, before I could find my words. "What happened? The demon—the cage—"

That image, the fiend flinging our trap away into the forest—had that really happened?

"You burned yourself down, pouring all that magic in," the medic said. "I've never seen anyone..." She paused and seemed to gather herself. "The demon was too strong. We had to retreat. It was close, but..."

"Close isn't enough," I filled in. My mouth curled in a grimace. We'd failed, again. *I'd* failed.

"You just worry about resting and recovering your spark now," the medic said grimly. "We may need you again sooner rather than later. The last hour, it's been picking up speed again. And it's heading straight for Portland now. At the rate it's moving... it might make it there tomorrow."

CHAPTER FOURTEEN

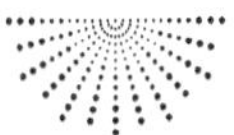

Gabriel

The hitch finally left Rose's breath about a half hour after we'd all climbed into the suite's master bed with her. She kept her head tucked against my chest, her fingers clamped around a fold in my shirt.

"I tried," she mumbled. "I tried so hard."

My chest squeezed. I stroked my hand over her hair, wishing I could wipe her pain away with that gesture. I could smell a hint of the grass she must have fallen into on her skin.

"I know," I said. "Of course you did."

Naomi and her mother had come with the enforcers who'd brought Rose back to the hotel. Our consort had been wobbly on her feet then—might still be now if she attempted to get up. Her cousin and aunt had told us what had happened in disjointed fragments as they pieced together the story between them, but it hadn't taken long to get the picture.

The plan with the trap had almost worked, but only almost. Rose had expended so much energy trying to push the demon into the cage that she'd fainted and been out cold for an hour before she'd come to. The witch medic had said she needed quiet and rest—*And when she's up for it, her spark will probably need stoking,* she'd added with a meaningful look at the five of us.

"It came close to working," Kyler said. He rubbed Rose's calf where he was sitting near the foot of the bed, his expression tensed with worry. "We could try again, build off what we saw this time—"

Rose shook her head. "We weren't strong enough. *I* wasn't strong enough." She swallowed audibly. "I could feel it, you know—the way the demon-ness in me could affect the demon. I gave everything, and it wasn't enough."

"It's not all on you," Seth said firmly. "The Assembly can gather more witches, add to their power that way."

"Our regular magic hardly touches it," Rose said. "It *is* on me. And I can't do it. Even if we could try the trap again... The way it's moving, it'll be here at the city before we could fix the cage and get everything together." She pressed closer to me. "It's coming here. How many people are going to die before this is over?"

I couldn't do anything except hug her. The hopelessness in her voice wrenched at me, but the same emotion filled the space between my ribs with a hollow ache. I didn't know how to fix this, how to stop that monster, either.

Damon scooted closer to Rose on her other side, kissing the back of her head. His arm tightened around her shoulders in a gesture I suspected only looked that possessive because I was the guy closest to him. He still hadn't really forgiven me for leaving—and, well, I wasn't sure I blamed him. I wasn't sure *I'd* completely forgiven myself for putting Rose through that much pain to carry out my plan.

All we could do now was move forward, though. So we stayed cuddled in a ring around her, offering her everything we could.

There might be more we could offer, as the medic had hinted. Jin clearly hadn't missed that insinuation. After Rose had relaxed into the mattress again, he trailed his fingers lightly over her thigh, smoothing the fabric of her sweatpants.

"It sounds like you drained yourself, Briar Rose," he said, his voice low. "If you need the full consort experience, just say the word." His smile came out a little crooked.

Rose barely stirred. "This is enough for now," she said. "My spark doesn't hurt anymore."

"If we gave you all the power *we* can," Ky started, but she was already shaking her head again.

"You did. I had everything I could have asked for, everything the bonds between us would allow. Every witch has her limits."

"No matter how eager her consorts are?" Damon asked suggestively, raising his eyebrow.

"Yes," she muttered, with enough good humor to elbow him in mock offense. But a second later her face had fallen again. I didn't know what was going on with the spark of magic inside her, but too much of her usual energy had gone out of her eyes.

Everything the bonds between us would allow. Her words traveled through my mind as I pressed my lips to her forehead. It tugged up memories from past conversations. An idea lit in my own head, so sudden and bright I had to hold myself back from sitting upright with a jerk.

Instead, I eased myself up and glanced around at the other guys. "Why don't we see what kind of dinner we can put together, then? And anything else that could make Rose even more comfortable while she's recovering."

"It's okay," Rose started, but I gave her a no-arguments look.

"We'll feel better if we're doing something. And you have to eat—that's not up for discussion."

The other guys started to move off the bed as I caught their eyes in turn, hoping my expression would clue them in that I had a bigger reason for calling us out of the room. Only Damon didn't budge.

"You can all figure that stuff out," he said, glowering at me. "I think I'm better off—"

I cut him off. "Damon, we're going to need you too. You're the take-out expert for this neighborhood now, aren't you?"

I kept my tone light, but the look I was giving him sharpened. Damon made a face. For a second, I thought he still hadn't gotten a clue and was going to insist on arguing more, but then he kissed Rose's cheek and pushed himself off the bed.

"I'll be right back, angel," he said.

He came out into the living room with the rest of us, scowling. "She needs us right now," he said, with at least enough self-control to keep his voice down. "We shouldn't be leaving her alone. I know you have all your great heroic plans, but—"

I held up my hand. "Damon. You're still pissed off at me. I get it. And I'm still sorry for how that all went down. But this *is* about Rose—about her needing us. Can you at least let me explain?"

His jaw worked, but he sank onto the arm of the sofa. "Make it quick."

"What are you thinking, Gabriel?" Seth asked, his forehead furrowed but his tone hopeful.

When we were kids, these guys had always looked to me to take the lead. I liked to think I'd never steered us all that wrong. But this—it was bigger than any of that. Still, the more the idea came together in my head, the more sure I was that it was the answer we needed.

I turned to Kyler. "You mentioned a while back that there's another type of consorting you read about when you were looking through the Assembly's files. A more permanent one?"

Ky nodded, studying me. "It doesn't look like it's done very often anymore—that's what Rose said too. The regular one, if one of the consorts isn't happy after the first few years, from what I've gathered they can 'divorce' and no one gets hurt. The 'soul-bound' ceremony I saw mentions of… Rose said it's unbreakable. You're bound together until you die."

"And when one of you dies, the other does too," I said. "I remember. She also said it means a deeper connection, more energy shared, didn't she?"

Understanding dawned on Ky's face. Jin let out a soft whistle.

"She said we can't give her more power with the bonds we have," I went on. "But if we had an even stronger bond, if we were even more closely connected…"

Damon pushed himself to his feet. "What the hell are we waiting for, then? Is there anyone here who isn't ready to commit that far?" He glanced around the group, on the verge of a glare as if anticipating a protest.

Jin laughed. "'Til death do us part. The way the last couple months have gone, we've pretty much already committed to that, haven't we? This'll just make it a bit more literal. I can handle that. You all just have to promise to live a long, long time, all right?"

Ky's eyes had brightened, but he paused with a frown. "It's not just about what we're ready for. I've brought it up with Rose a couple of times now, and she's always dismissed the idea right away. She wouldn't even consider it." A shadow crossed his face. "She's afraid we'll end up regretting it."

"She's got to believe now that we know what we're in for," Seth said. "If we're still here after being chased across the country and threatened by demons, we're here."

"She's not getting rid of us," Damon said with a dark grin.

"Then we just have to convince her of that," I said. "That's why I wanted to talk to you all first, to make sure we're all sure, before I brought it up to her. She has to see how much this means to us too."

A new part of the idea started to unfurl in my head. Even though I was worried about convincing Rose, a smile touched my lips. "I think I might know exactly how to put it to her."

* * *

Rose was still curled up on the bed when we returned, but she eased into a sitting position at the sound of the door. She took us in as we filed through the doorway.

"No dinner?" she said, her slight teasing smile not quite reaching her clouded eyes.

"We can get to that in a little bit," I said. "There's something more important we need to say first. Come here?"

I beckoned her to the edge of the bed. The five of us had come to a stop in a row there. As soon as she'd scooted close, we all went down on bended knee, each of us reaching for her closest hand in unison. My fingers closed around hers alongside Seth's and Kyler's.

"Rose Hallowell," I said. "Would you do us the honor of making us your soul-bound consorts?"

She was already staring at us. At those words, her cheeks flushed red. She started to tug back her hands. "I can't ask you to make that kind of commitment when—"

"Rose." I squeezed her hand, and she stilled. "You're not asking. We are. We understand the risks. We've already staked our lives on being with you, Sprout. Can't you see that? None of us cares how many witches are trying to kill us or which monsters are looking to rend our souls apart—we'll still want to be with you. We're at our best together. And I can't wait to find out what that best looks like when we're *not* under constant attack."

"Me neither," Jin murmured.

"It's going to be fucking spectacular," Damon said.

"For once, Damon and I see completely eye to eye," Seth put in with a smile.

"I'd just like to point out that this was my idea *months* ago," Kyler said. "Just so we know where credit is due. Oh, and I don't have any more doubts now than I did then. Which means none."

Rose's lips twitched upward. "I didn't want it to be like this," she said. "I didn't want you to ever have to be in danger."

"What's life without some danger?" I said. "And it's not just us now. If that demon goes on a real rampage, if the other ones get loose too, the whole world's in trouble. You pushed yourself to the brink out there trying to stop that from happening. You've got to let us take some risks too. Even if it's hard for me to see deepening the connection we have as some kind of risk."

She drew in a breath. Her hand trembled in ours. "It still might not be enough. You might make that sacrifice and we still can't save anyone."

"It's not a *sacrifice* to be your consort in any way we can," Damon said. "It would be an honor. You know I wouldn't say that if I didn't mean it."

"As long as *you're* sure you'd want to make that kind

of commitment yourself," Seth started, and a choked laugh escaped Rose's lips.

"The five of you—you've always felt like home," she said. "When we were kids, all the time I spent with you, it was the only time I ever got to be completely myself. Every day that we were apart, I missed that feeling. I missed you and who I could be with you. If I'd thought it was possible back then, I'd have been ready years ago. I just want to do what's best for you."

"I think what's best for us is kicking some demon ass —or at least, watching the love of our lives do that with all the strength we can give you." Kyler straightened up and touched Rose's cheek. "We're in this. One hundred percent."

Seth nodded. "You always want people to be able to make their own choices—this is ours. You just have to accept it."

A liquid gleam shone in Rose's eyes. I released her hand so she could swipe at them. "Spark help me. I don't know how I got lucky enough to find all of you, and then find you again. Of course. I can't think of anything that would make me happier."

CHAPTER FIFTEEN

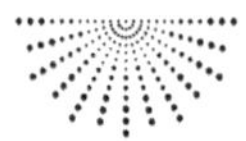

Rose

The garden behind Thalia's estate house on the outskirts of Portland was a little wild—I couldn't tell how much by accident or by design. Between the winding hedges, flowers that some people might have called weeds dappled the overgrown but soft grass. A blooming vine looped up and over the central ring of shrubs. The nearest tree bowed close, its branches gnarled but its leaves bright green. A sweet scent, both floral and mossy, carried in the warm early morning air.

I drank that air deep into my lungs. "It's perfect," I said to Thalia. "Are you sure..."

I didn't know how to finish that question. I suspected it was in this garden that Thalia would have taken her former husband as consort—the consort who'd fed her magic to the demons. She'd told me she could help us carry out the soul-bond ceremony, that she'd studied the rituals before out of curiosity, but I hadn't realized until right now just how painful participating might be for her.

"I can't think of anything better that could happen in this space," the older witch said now, turning to me with a gentle smile. "My home should have had more love in it. You and your men can bring some back to it. Make it a place where maybe I could see finding another love of my own, a true one, someday."

When she put it that way, I couldn't argue. "All right then." I smoothed my hands over the silky fabric of my dress, a new one I'd had to buy for this purpose, since there hadn't been time to drive home and raid my wardrobe for a suitable outfit. Instead of the pale gold that was traditional for the regular consorting ceremony, this one was pure white. Symbolic of the total openness, the dissolving of all boundaries, that a soul-bound consorting meant. "How do we start?"

"I'll need to arrange the supplies," Thalia said. "It should only take a few minutes. Why don't you and your consorts get settled in here while you wait. Everything will go more smoothly the more comfortable you feel."

Maybe it would have been better if we could have returned to the Hallowell estate, then. On the other hand, my family home came with a lot of mixed memories. The joyful times when I'd roamed the grounds with the guys as kids, sure. I'd never forget the ecstasy of our first consorting ceremony in those woods either.

But it was also the place where my father had manipulated my mother until her death, where he'd lied to me and tried to ensnare me. It was the place where I'd had to fend off not one but two false consorts-to-be.

No, being here, in this place brand new to all of us, seemed like the right decision. Which was a good thing, because we didn't have time to change course now. We were doing this out of love, but not just for each other. It was for all the fellow human beings our strengthened bond might help me save as well.

Thalia went to grab the supplies she'd brought, and I left the circle of hedges to find the guys. They were ambling through the grounds, looking more at ease than they had for most of the last week. We'd gotten more traditional consorting clothes for them too: light shirts and loose trousers, all as white as my dress. It was a little strange seeing them dressed as if they were witching men, but the sight sent a tickle of affection through me too.

Gabriel came over to me first, the deep auburn of his hair even darker in the thin dawn light. He took my hand, raised it to his lips, and kissed my knuckles—easily, without a second's hesitation. The affection in me swelled into an ache.

"No second thoughts?" I said—with a smile, but I meant the question too. Gabriel hadn't been consorted to me the regular way for anywhere near as long as the other four guys. He felt like an ineffable part of our group, and he'd taken his usual place within our circle of friendship after just a few minutes of arriving back in town, but he couldn't ever have imagined he'd be taking a step like this.

"Not one," he said. "You know..." His gaze traveled

across the other guys, who were starting to make their way over. "I think I've been missing the sense of having a family for a long time. After my mom left, after my dad fell apart... The last few months, it's the first time I've felt like I was really part of something bigger, something good." His fingers tightened around mine. "Knowing I'm going to have this forever, or at least as long as I live? I couldn't imagine anything better."

A lump rose in my throat. I touched his jaw to draw him into a kiss. He kissed me back tenderly, but with the hot slide of his hand down my side like a promise of things to come.

Thalia had assured me that the center of the garden was completely private. When she finished the ceremony and retreated to the house, we wouldn't have to worry about any spectators as our new bond fully took hold.

"Hey!" Damon said. "Aiming to get a head start?" When I turned to mock-glower at him, he grinned. Ever since I'd accepted their proposal yesterday evening, he'd seemed looser, less wound-up. The thought struck me with a pang: Maybe up until now some part of him had still been a little worried that I might not keep him with me. Damon knew how to put on a tough front, but I'd seen how vulnerable he could be underneath.

"I suppose I'll just have to kiss all of you to make it even," I said, arching my eyebrows. "Poor me."

He laughed and swooped in to make good on that suggestion. I gripped the collar of his shirt and kissed him back hard, as if he'd need more convincing of how much I meant it.

"All right, love birds," Thalia said, sounding amused, as she returned. "We're ready to begin."

The six of us followed her back to the center of the garden. "You'd think a ceremony like this should be terribly complicated," she said. "But especially with you all already bonded with each other, it's really quite simple. Mostly it depends on the willingness and emotion inside you. If you can't open yourself up and accept the connection, it won't form."

"Okay," I said. My own worries had faded, but it was still good to know there was some sort of a safeguard in place. No one could enter this sort of consorting unless they were completely sure.

She arranged the guys in a ring with me in the center. The grass between us was carved with glyphs. Crisply herbal incense smoke drifted from the sticks she'd set burning around the border of hedges.

"You remember the form I had you practice last night?" she said. "We'll take it one at a time, each of you passing Rose on to the next. When it's time for the clasping of hands, you'll need to pause for me to bring the dagger. Speak when I prompt you to. That's all there is to it. I'll begin."

Thalia stepped back and spun on her feet in a slow circle, her arms drawing patterns through the air. "The Spark that guides us, bless this partnering," she said in a lilting voice that echoed through my bones. "Let souls that long to unite be one, so that they may honor you that much more. Let love and light flow freely, between Rose Hallowell and Kyler Lennox. Hear them now."

"I open my soul to you," I said, holding Ky's gaze.

"Let every light shine between us."

A smile that looked almost giddy had stretched across my consort's face. "I open my soul to you. Let every light shine between us."

We'd gone through the brief form enough times last night, all of us, that I barely needed to think. He reached toward me and I looped my arm around his. We whirled around each other, twining tighter and then easing apart. Our hands slid down each other's arms until our palms nearly touched. My spark swayed in my chest with an eager heat.

Thalia stepped up to us with her ritual silver dagger gleaming in her hands. She slipped it between our not-quite-joined hands and nicked our palms with the faintest sting. I pressed my blood to Kyler's.

The flame of magic inside me billowed out with a glow that felt like liquid sunlight streaming through my veins. My breath caught. From the shine in Ky's eyes, he must have felt something like that too.

"Their souls entwined, from this breath to the last," Thalia intoned.

"Our souls entwined, from this breath to the last," Ky and I said together. A jolt like a tiny bolt of lightning shot between our hands—and sent that wonderous glow spiking down to my core.

We spun around each other again, slipping past each other's limbs, our hands staying melded together. With each brush of Ky's body against mine, the heat inside me blazed hotter and purer. At the end, with our clasped hands hugged between our chests, we brought our mouths together. His kiss seared my lips.

If it'd been only us two, the ceremony would have ended now, and we could have taken each other in every possible way. Instead, I tamped down on that tug of desire and turned. Ky swung me under his arm toward Jin.

"Let souls that long to unite be one," Thalia said. "Let love and light flow freely, between Rose Hallowell and Jin Lyang. Hear them now."

We said the words and stepped into our form. Jin moved with me as gracefully as if he'd been born to this dance. His face glowed as our hands came together and Thalia drew fresh blood from our palms. The white-hot light of my spark tingled through me at a higher pitch. When we spun around each other again, I barely felt my feet touching the ground.

With each of the guys, with each promise exchanged, with each kiss, the rush of brilliant energy inside me flowed faster. I reached Gabriel last, my nerves singing, my skin ablaze as if I contained a sun within me. The awe in his expression would have destroyed any fears I had left if his earlier comments hadn't already.

The actual sun was beaming over the tops of the hedges now. It gleamed off Thalia's silver-streaked hair as she brought her dagger to bear one last time. "Their souls entwined, from this breath to the last," she said.

"Our souls entwined, from this breath to the last," Gabriel said with me. His love shone right back at me, so clear it was hard to believe I'd ever thought he'd lost it.

The rising tide of longing swelled as we completed the movements of our form. Gabriel's free hand skimmed my waist, and I almost whimpered just at that brief contact. I caught a glimpse of Thalia's smile as she slipped away between the hedges, leaving us to our joining. And then it was only us six.

Gabriel claimed my mouth with the same urgency ringing through me. I clung to him, trembling with need. When our lips parted, I found the wherewithal to gasp out, "All of us united. Let love and light flow freely."

My consorts came to me. Desire blazed between us, so brightly I could barely tell where I ended and they began. Lips pressed to my neck and a thumb teased over the peak of my breast and fingers glided up my thigh, raising my dress. I gave myself over to them, to every sensation rippling through me, to the connection that streamed between us as easily as the thump of our heartbeats, the eager rasp of our breaths.

My dress fell to the ground, the sun warm on my bare skin. As two of the guys tugged down my panties, I nudged Kyler down on the crumpled fabric. Somewhere in the haze of wanting, I'd stripped off his shirt. The lean muscles in his chest flexed as he wriggled out of his pants. The head of his cock slid over my sex as I arched against him.

"Rose," he murmured. He cupped the back of my head, pushing himself up to embrace me as I pushed down onto him, welcoming him into me. His groan was lost in the meeting of our mouths. At that deeper physical connection, the blaze soared higher, from the top of my head to the soles of my feet. I rocked against him, and he bucked to meet me.

Other hands stroked over my breasts from behind. Ky eased back and thrust up again, each pulse of his cock making me moan as he stretched me, filled me. I was already so close—but I wanted all of them. I *needed* all of them.

My hand closed around the waist of Seth's pants. He wrenched them off in an instant, and I drew his erection into my mouth. He swore breathlessly, his fingertips grazing my scalp as he held me to him. Damon was kissing my neck. Gabriel reached down to stroke my clit just above the spot where I was joined with Ky.

My body shuddered, and the surge of pleasure blanked out my vision. I came braced against Ky's lean chest and Seth's hard thigh.

"I love you," Ky said, gripping my hip. "So much, Rose. So much." Then his head tipped back with the impact of his own release.

I sucked Seth down harder, and he came too with another groan. The aftershock of my orgasm and the flood of musky fluid in my mouth wasn't nearly enough. But my guys weren't done either.

Damon lifted me off Ky with such a gentle touch my heart sang even as desire made me grind against him. He and Gabriel caught me between them. Gabriel kissed me hard on the mouth while Damon slicked his tongue from the crook of my jaw to my earlobe with an electric quiver of bliss. As if they understood each other perfectly, Gabriel sank down, holding my hips steady, as Damon eased his cock into me from behind. As he filled me with one smooth thrust, Gabriel pressed his lips to my clit.

A cry escaped me. Then Jin was there, fondling my breasts and capturing my mouth as the other two guys sent me spiraling higher into ecstasy inside and out. My legs wobbled, but they held me. The light inside me pulsed alongside the rhythm our bodies made: Damon plunging deeper, Gabriel teasing my clit with the tips of his teeth, Jin swallowing my moans as he tweaked both nipples with expert fingers.

"Fuck," Damon muttered through his teeth, but he couldn't hold back his release. He hugged me tight as a hot spurt flooded me. I was close again, teetering on the edge of a maelstrom of passion, every nerve jittering with the love and light we shared.

Jin caught me, easing me down onto my dress on the grassy ground. I pulled him to me. As he plunged into my sex, bringing back the pressure I was craving, I tugged Gabriel closer too. A rumble escaped his throat as I palmed his cock. He bent over to kiss me with a stutter of breath.

With a few more thrusts, Jin's length found the perfect angle to send me flying. I gasped against Gabriel's mouth. My grip on his cock tightened, and he came hot and slick over my forearm. At his groan of bliss, I reached my peak. My toes curled as the blaze of pleasure radiated through every inch of me from my core. Jin came with me, bowing over me to claim one last kiss.

The six of us sprawled together in a haphazard version of our earlier ring, every one of my consorts with me skin to skin. In those first few moments, as our passion settled from a bonfire to a steady but heady burn, none of us spoke. But we didn't need to. Their joy hummed through me as clearly as my own.

I was theirs and they were mine, down to our very souls.

Rose

The closer we got to downtown Portland, the more the afterglow of the ceremony faded. I snuggled closer to Seth in the backseat of the car, breathing in his warm bronze-y scent and reveling in the tingle of bright energy that passed between us just with that innocuous contact. He hugged me closer with his arm around my shoulders. At my other side, Jin rubbed my knee.

My spark burned to hide away with my five consorts and bask in our newly strengthened bond all day, all week. The ache ran even deeper than when we'd first committed to each other. But if we gave in to that impulse, the demon might have ravaged the city around us by the time we emerged.

I didn't know if I could summon enough power now to overcome that monster, but I could feel I had more.

The magic humming through my chest with each sway of my spark had a stark brilliance to it that I'd never felt before. My spark wasn't just a flame now but a miniature star.

We hadn't heard any news about the demon while we'd been on Thalia's estate, but the Assembly wouldn't necessarily have reached out to her or me at this point. Who knew what destruction it might have wrought in the last few hours? My stomach knotted at the thought.

When the car pulled up outside the Assembly building, I took a small comfort in the fact that the building *was* still standing, and all the ones around it on the street too. The medic yesterday had said at its current pace, the demon might reach the city later today. Steeling myself, I climbed out of the car with the guys. The rest of my consorts spilled out of the second car that had been driving with us.

The gray face of the Assembly building loomed over us, looking solemn and impenetrable. I motioned my consorts to me. "Come on. Let's talk to them together. They're going to have to start accepting us as a package deal, especially now." And the idea of my newly soul-bonded partners traveling even blocks away from me down the street made my heart wrench.

We filed into the building. Thalia gave my hand a squeeze and moved down the hall to check in with the other recovering witches. I turned to one of the enforcers on guard near the doors.

"Are the Northcotts in their office?"

"Lady Northcott is on the premises," she said. Her eyes slid over the guys, with a wariness I couldn't help noticing. How many times had we come and gone from this building in the last week, and that tension remained.

I guessed that was as good an answer as I was going to get. We headed up the stairs to the Northcotts' office on the fifth and top floor. The building might look modern enough, but witching society hadn't thought elevators worth bothering with. It really was ridiculous how much so many of them looked down on the unsparked when we had plenty of backwards habits ourselves.

Lady Northcott was sitting at her desk when we pushed into the office. Her secretary startled, but the head of the Assembly made a reassuring gesture, and he settled back in his station near the door. She took in me and my consorts with an inscrutable expression.

"You're looking well, Lady Hallowell," she said. "I'm glad to see yesterday's efforts haven't set you back too far."

"I'm sorry I wasn't able to contribute more," I said, with a fresh pang of guilt thinking of my failure yesterday. "I'll be more prepared next time. What's the current status of the demon?"

She frowned, glancing at the phone sitting face-up on her desk in a way that made me suspect she'd recently gotten an update from the observers in the field. "It's continued cutting a path straight toward Portland. Not very quickly, but still faster than before. It looks likely to reach the suburbs sometime tonight if we can't redirect it."

"What are your plans at this point?"

Her mouth tightened. "We're still discussing the

options. Our first two gambits seemed like our best bets. We were able to retrieve some pieces of the cage, but they were damaged—it looks unlikely we could have them in working order in time, if we could even hope a second attempt might work."

"I can get in there and start helping with that as soon as we're done here," Seth said. "If that's where you think I'd be most needed."

My spirits had lifted. We had some time; we could make this work. "I think we *can* hope a second attempt would go better," I said. "We came right to you so you know—my consorts and I took the soul-bond this morning. My spark has never shone brighter. I can't promise I'm strong enough now to push back the demon as much as we need, but I'll have a much better chance of it."

My voice faltered on the last few words. Lady Northcott's whole face had gone rigid, her gaze fixed on me in a stare that looked almost horrified.

"You did *what*?" she said in a low choked voice.

I'd expected perhaps some surprise and maybe raised eyebrows at my decision, but not this distress. "We conducted the soul-bound consorting ceremony, with Lady Ainsworth's help," I said, as if there was any way she could have misunderstood my meaning. My right hand turned outward instinctively, displaying the scar like a tiny starburst on my palm where Thalia had healed the dagger's scratch. "The magic we'll be able to create together now is purer, stronger—I can already tell I'll be able to do more. Withstand more."

Lady Northcott pushed to her feet, the wheels of her

desk chair rattling over the linoleum floor. She motioned me to a door at the back of the room, the entrance to her magicking room. "I think we'd better talk just the two of us, witch to witch."

My legs balked. "My consorts are my equals in this decision," I said. "I wouldn't be here without them."

"Nonetheless," Northcott said, "I would speak with you alone. Consider it a direct order from the highest position in the Assembly. Are you refusing that order?"

The crispness of her tone suggested that if I did, I'd find a host of enforcers taking the decision out of my hands. I swallowed hard.

"No. But I follow it under protest."

"Noted," she said dryly, and swept her arm for me to come.

"We'll be right here if you need us," Gabriel said, both a promise and the closest he could get to a warning for Lady Northcott.

The magicking room for the head of the Assembly looked pretty similar to mine back home: pale hardwood floor, blank white walls without a single window, a single clear light fixture on the ceiling. A hint of cedar incense lingered in the air. Instead of a cabinet, hers had a built-in cupboard. Northcott didn't make any move toward it, though. We weren't in here to cast a spell. The soundproofed walls to prevent distraction would also keep my consorts and her secretary from overhearing our conversation.

"What were you thinking?" she snapped, spinning to face me the moment the door had closed with a thud.

"The soul-bound ceremony, with not one but *five* unsparked men?"

I'd already been tense, but at her words I bristled even more. "We were *thinking* that the only thing that stopped us from caging the demon was my power faltering. It won't falter as soon now. We're committed to each other. We all knew what we were getting into."

Lady Northcott made a jerky motion with her hand. "There's a proper process for any consorting. A department to consult with, approval you're supposed to gain first. Especially in the case of a higher form."

I hadn't even thought of that. I shouldn't have laughed, but the sound spilled out of me before I could catch it. Was that all she was worried about? Whether we'd filled out the proper forms?

"I didn't have approval to consort with them in the first place," I said. "Circumstances made that impossible, in case you've forgotten. Strangely enough, we thought finding the strength to push back the demon was more important than getting some paperwork filed."

"They're bound to the entire witching community now," Northcott went on, ignoring the point I'd made. "There's never been a soul-bound consorting with an unsparked man before."

"How do you know? We have no idea how many records have been destroyed, evidence covered up. Have you even looked into who else in the Assembly might have been supporting *those* efforts, even if they didn't know about the demons?" It wasn't hard to imagine all sorts of witches and witching men might have wanted to encourage a more restricted view of consorting—out of ideas of purity, or control, or who knew what else.

"No," Lady Northcott said tightly. "We've been rather occupied with the demon problem."

"Exactly!" I gestured toward the doorway, to the guys waiting on the other side. "So let us help fix that problem. I'll do whatever I can. My consorts, unsparked or not, care just as much as anyone here. You've got no reason to distrust them."

Northcott's eyes narrowed. "What makes you think I'm most concerned with trusting them? This consorting was based on your judgment. You have the demon's taint in you, and you've brought yourself even more power."

A chill ran down my back. So this wasn't just about unsparked prejudice then. She was still wary of *me*.

"I can't help that," I said, my voice dropping. "It happened before I was even born, Lady Northcott. But I've never done one thing to hurt anyone who wasn't already attacking me. Your own enforcers can tell you how close we were to capturing the demon yesterday, how much I put into that effort. Maybe that power is a weapon, but I decide how I use it, and there's no taint in my mind."

She gazed back at me, frowning, as if she weren't entirely sure she believed that. Then she sighed and folded her arms over her chest. "I suppose it is what it is now. You can't take back the binding."

"No, I can't," I said. "So are you going to let us help or not?"

Her lips pursed. She inclined her head. "Move back into the office we set up for the six of you here. We may need to call on you without much notice. Your consorts can continue contributing however they were before. You... For now, why don't you look in on the witches who were caught up in this faction. It seems you've made some progress with them. They have the experience— they may be the ones to shift the balance."

"They're traumatized," I said. "If we ask too much of them too quickly, we'll just open those wounds more before they've had a chance to heal."

"They won't heal at all if the demon gets its claws into them," Lady Northcott retorted. "You wanted to help. That's how I'll accept your help right now."

She grasped the doorknob without waiting for my answer. I let her usher me back into the main office space. My consorts were standing where I'd left them, Damon scowling, Kyler's gaze searching as if he were trying to read the outcome of that talk from my face.

I caught both their hands, and all five of us slipped into the hall. "Rose?" Seth said, sounding concerned. I guessed my face wasn't completely unreadable.

"She's not happy," I said. "But she's at least letting us return to the things we were doing to help before. Not that they're sure any of it will do much good." I raked my fingers through my hair. "I don't think anyone in this building has a clue how we're going to stop that fiend."

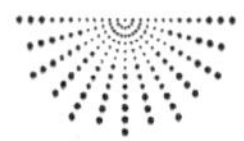

CHAPTER SEVENTEEN

Jin

Rose had said she needed to go, but she wavered by the door to our Assembly office after that announcement, her mouth twisted with uncertainty. I moved to her side automatically, reaching for her hand and twining my fingers through hers.

"You don't have to do what Lady Northcott said," I reminded her. "It's not as if these heads of witching society have had the answers before now."

"I know," she said. "But I *should* see what I can do for the witches in recovery. And honestly, I agree with her. It might be so much easier if they could stand beside us against that thing. I just hate to ask it of them."

"So you won't," I said. "You'll help them find their strength, and when they're strong enough that they can handle it, of course they'll want to pitch in. They've already said that, haven't they?"

The corners of her lips curled upward until I had a real smile. "How do you always know how to find the bright side of a situation, Jin?"

I shrugged, grinning back. "Just my special talent. You can't be an artist unless you know how to look at things from all the different angles."

A shadow crossed her face again. "I wish the Assembly wasn't looking at us from the cynical angle they've picked." She shook her head. "They'll shun me for having you, and you for being with me. It can't get any more tangled than that."

"Ah, who needs them, anyway? We defeat this demon and then say sayonara to the bunch of them. We do just fine when it's only the six of us."

In a sort of demonstration, I raised her hand and twirled her around beneath my arm, like one of the moves in the consorting ritual's form. A soft laugh escaped Rose's lips as her hair fanned out with the movement. A glow had formed behind my ribs during that ceremony, and it quivered happily at the sound.

I'd felt connected to Rose from the moment of our first consorting, but this new bond... I wasn't sure how much I even believed in souls, but I could feel the energy that flowed between us now like a gentle wash of light, illuminating and filling every lonely place I might have had left inside me.

Beautiful. Like watching the sun rise over the ruins of an ancient city with all the colors flaring into vividness, except it stayed. It wasn't just a single spectacular moment, but a constant I'd be able to count on as long as we both lived.

"I'll be in the same building the whole time," she said. "And I'll come back as soon as I can. I... don't like the feeling of being apart from you all right now."

"We did this for a reason," I said. "And part of that reason is so you can find ways to kick demon butt—ways that we probably can't help with. Do what you need to do."

She bobbed up for a quick kiss that sent fresh warmth through the glow of our bond, and then she ducked out. I turned back to my fellow consorts.

Kyler had dropped straight into the chair at the desk, setting the laptop he'd grabbed from our hotel suite into its former position. From the hazy look in his eyes, he was already immersed in the files. Seth had spread some of his blueprints on the other side of the desk, leaning over as he frowned at them. Gabriel, standing nearby, shot me an approving smile when our eyes met. I suspected he'd been listening to my conversation with Rose.

Damon stalked from one end of the office to the other. His jaw had been clenched since Lady Northcott had ushered Rose away from us with disapproval that couldn't have been more obvious. Now his back was rigid too.

"We can't let them get away with this," he said. "We're supposed to stand by Rose, so let's fucking do it. These assholes can't shove her off to the side after everything she's done for them, just because they don't like *us*."

"They gave us the office back," Gabriel said mildly. "Lady Northcott told Rose how she'd like her to help. I'm not sure they have any better ideas for what any of us can be doing."

"Then they should be listening to us, to Rose!" Damon said with a slash of his hand. "Hell, I could come up with better plans in two seconds than they've managed so far. Maybe we should track down some heavy firepower. Guns might not do the trick, but I could probably figure out who to go to if we wanted some missile launchers or shit like that. Let's see the demon face off against those."

Seth looked up at him with an eyebrow raised. "There are some ways to solve problems that don't involve blowing them up," he said, and turned back to his blueprints. "Maybe I can find a method to strengthen the cage even more... Or disguise it somehow. It doesn't do us any good unless they can move the demon onto it and then into it. There's got to be something I've missed."

"I can take another look at them too," I offered. "Sometimes a fresh pair of eyes..."

He nodded with a grateful glance my way. "I appreciate that, Jin. Although I think I'd better handle any final adjustments. Maybe one of the other workers slipped up without me noticing. We've got to be so careful with this." He rubbed his mouth.

"With all these records of the faction's dealings with the demons, you'd think there'd be something else in here we could work with." Ky grimaced at the laptop's screen, his fingers flying over the keyboard. "If I could get into the private areas of the Assembly network—of course, they'll be even more pissed off with us if I hack in."

"You don't think they'd let you in if you asked?" Gabriel said.

Ky shook his head. "Already did. They weren't comfortable with it. Said there couldn't be anything in there that'd relate to the demons anyway, since they never even knew the demons existed. I just want to know everything there is to know about the community, about magic—the more I understand, the more it'll all come together."

"What do they care about what you might see in there?" Damon said. He came to an abrupt stop in the middle of the room. "There's a fucking monster on the horizon and they're too busy looking down their noses at us to give us the tools we need to fight it. If I could just give those smug pricks a piece of my mind—"

Gabriel clapped his hands, straightening up into an authoritative posture. "We'll work with what we have. We've made it through plenty of horrible situations in the past with a lot less than we've got now. We just keep working to our strengths, and there'll be an answer somewhere."

His words jarred loose something in me. For a second, it felt as if the glow inside me had seared right up to my eyes. I blinked, taking in the room, the four guys I'd known since we were little kids, and all I could see was how predictable this all was.

There was Kyler, digging up every fact he could. There was Seth, plotting a thoughtful careful course. There was Damon, trying to slam and blast his way through the mess. And Gabriel, always the leader, trying to corral us.

But maybe this wasn't the right corral. Were we playing to our strengths or just stuck in a rut? We'd been spinning our wheels just like this for days, and the demon was still out there. Rose still felt that stopping it rested on her shoulders alone.

The realization struck me like a jab to the gut. Words collected and jarred in my throat. Who the hell was I to tell the rest of them they were doing things wrong?

Oh. That was my rut, wasn't it? Jin the optimist. Going with the flow, letting the worries roll off my back, always looking on the bright side, like Rose had said.

Maybe it was time I pointed out some other sides to this situation. If I wanted to see us all out of our ruts, I had to start with myself. Even if the thought of criticizing my best friends to their faces made me wince inwardly.

I squared my shoulders. Damon was just launching into some more of his rant. "We've got to stop letting them push us around. We have to *demand* we get what we need. March right back into that office and—"

"No," I said, loud enough that my voice filled the room. I did wince then. But the gazes of the other four guys snapped to me, startled, and I knew I'd gotten their attention. I forced myself to keep going.

"Look at us," I said. "We're doing the same old things we always do. Approaching this problem the same old ways. But it's not enough. Can't you see that?"

"What are you saying, Jin?" Gabriel said, quietly but without any hostility.

"Just that—Rose is pushing herself to her limits, stretching herself in ways she never had to before, to tackle this thing. Because it's not like anything we've ever had to tackle before. If we want to support her, we've got to do the same thing. Think outside the boxes we're comfortable in. Look at what's really happening and where we can make a difference even if it's hard—with eyes wide open, without any blinders. Stop running in circles we already know haven't gotten us anywhere."

For several seconds, the others kept staring at me. Then Ky let his hands come to rest on the desk. "You're right," he said. "I'm just covering the same ground over and over again here."

"So what does that mean?" Damon demanded, but even he looked a little subdued compared to his earlier furor. "What exactly should we do?"

"I don't know," I admitted. "I just think it needs to be different. Bigger. Better. Maybe... Maybe we need to start by getting out of this room and actually interacting more with these Assembly people. They're the ones Rose has to be working with. We're pissed off that they don't respect us, but we haven't encouraged much of an alliance between us either, have we?"

"No," Gabriel said grimly. "We haven't."

Seth pushed away from his blueprints. "I'll find out which of the officials are overseeing the cage reconstruction and start from there." He glanced at me. "Did you want to come with, or...?"

"I think that's as good a starting point as any," I said. The glow in me ebbed again, but the flicker of it was more buoyant now. More hopeful. "I'll just have to see where I can get to from there."

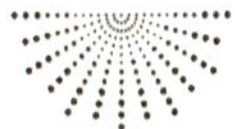

CHAPTER EIGHTEEN

Rose

Normally when I ventured into the side hall where the Assembly had set up rooms for the recovering witches I was met by only quiet stillness and maybe some murmured voices. The women who until recently had been virtual slaves to their consorts and the demons weren't really the boisterous sort. So my heart started beating faster the moment I heard footsteps rushing over the floor. A sharp sobbing carried all the way to the stairs. I hurried out of the stairwell and around the bend.

Thalia was hustling between one of the rooms and another, her brown-and-silver hair flying astray, her frown digging furrows at the corners of her mouth. She stopped when she saw me, one hand on the doorframe. The sobbing was fading, but someone else was speaking in a low frantic babble I couldn't make out much of.

"What's going on?" I said.

"Word went around that the demon is coming toward the city," she said. "That it looks like it'll be here soon. And if that wasn't frightening enough, I think some of the witches most recently in contact with them can already feel its approach. They weren't ready. It's brought a lot of the fear and anguish back up. I'm doing what I can."

"Are you okay?"

She nodded with a jerk of her chin. "I've had a few weeks longer to get my head on straight compared to everyone else here. A good thing, I suppose. Not that I'm pleased about the news, but I'll cope."

She slipped into the room, and I followed. The space had been set up like my and the guys' room upstairs, with six cots in two rows. Lesley was already inside, kneeling next to one of the cots where Eloise was sitting, hunched over and hugging her knees. The middle-aged witch had her gnarled hands clenched together in front of her calves, and her shoulders quivered, but she was quiet right now. Lesley wove patterns in the air over her back at a soothing rhythm.

Thalia made for a bed in the corner, where Crystal was perched with her head in her hands. The young witch was muttering a jumbled stream of words, none of which strung together to make any sense that I could decipher. "The Cliff—they would—if it sees—feel it now —can't stay—where—coming, coming—I wanted—oh—"

"Hey, now," Thalia said in a soft voice, sitting next to Crystal. She squeezed the other witch's shoulder and then moved her hands in a calming spell of her own.

Crystal's muttering slowed, but Eloise started crying again with hitches of breath. Across the hall, someone let out a brief thin shriek.

The other two witches who were in this room looked all right, if unnerved. I darted to the second dorm room. Caroline's bright blond head was bent next to Selena's, the elderly witch rubbing red-rimmed eyes. Caroline cast an uncertain glance toward a younger woman who'd pressed herself against the opposite wall.

"It wants us," the other witch said, in a thready voice that made me suspect she was the one who'd shrieked. "It won't stop until it's completely consumed us."

I skirted the cots to reach her, taking her hand in mine. This situation didn't require the same sort of magicking as the kind I'd been working with the recovering witches before, but I knew forms for relaxing, for settling nerves. And there was plain old human comfort. I squeezed her fingers in what I hoped was a reassuring grip and looped my arm through the air to draw a shimmer of calm down over both of us. Because I was going to need plenty of fortification to be at my best too.

"We're not going to let it hurt any of you," I said in my most confident voice. "Every witch in the country will stand up to protect you. It *won't* have you. I swear it." And if I broke that promise, it'd be over my dead body.

The witch bowed her head, her breath still coming out ragged. "You don't know what it's like. You haven't felt it the way I have."

I hadn't and yet I also had. I knew what it was like to taste the essence of that monster from the inside out.

"I know how far we're willing to go to stop it from getting to you again," I said. "We can beat it." *We just have to figure out how.*

She didn't look completely convinced. On one of the other beds, another witch rolled over and buried her face in the pillow. A tremor ran through her body. My gaze locked with Caroline's where she was still sitting with Selena. Caroline didn't speak, but her wide eyes asked enough of a question on their own. *How in the name of the Spark could we help all of them even now?*

Inspiration tickled through my thoughts. "There are magicking supplies down here, aren't there?" I said. "Get me powdered lavender and chalk—whoever's up to it."

A witch near the door hustled out. I kept weaving my spell of calm around the woman with me until the other witch returned. I grabbed the bag of purple-gray powder from her and motioned Caroline over.

"Mark glyphs on the floor around all the beds," I told her. "Protection and easy sleep. Tie them together if you can."

Caroline nodded, her eyes gleaming nervously, and accepted the chalk. As she crouched down to start drawing, I pulled out a handful of the lavender powder. Its dry pungent scent filled my nose. I set the bag with the rest of its contents down by the wall and stepped into a larger form.

My feet carried me from the foot of one bed to the next, around Caroline and her hastily drawn glyphs, the movements partly drawn from forms I'd learned under my tutors' eyes and partly coming together on instinct. The brilliant light of my spark flooded my limbs as I moved, as if eager to bring my intentions into reality. My arms swayed with my magicking dance, wisps of lavender powder slipping through my fingers.

Let peace settle over this room, I thought, willing that hope into every gesture, every step. *Let their thoughts settle and their bodies quiet. Let them drift off into sleep if that's the soothing they need—a soft soothing sleep. Let nothing touch them—not fear or pain or the claws of an enemy.*

A stillness crept through the room, silence falling over us. Nothing reached my ears except the whisper of my feet over the floor and the faint rasp of the chalk as Caroline drew the last few glyphs. Selena leaned back on her hands, her white hair streaming down, the tension in her face seeping away.

The witch by the wall sank onto her cot and curled up there, her eyes drifting shut. The one who'd clung to her pillow rolled onto her side. Her gaze followed my movements dreamily.

I spun one more time after Caroline finished the last glyph, and then I eased to a stop. My own limbs felt comfortingly heavy, as if they'd been wrapped in a cozy blanket. The worried sympathy that had wrenched through me minutes ago had melted into sorrow-tinged relief.

Caroline straightened up, her stance more relaxed now too.

"We should do the magicking in the other room too," I said. "They all need some peace."

"I'm just glad we can do something," she said.

I snatched up the bag of lavender powder and ran into Thalia in the hall. "Good thinking with that spell," she said. "I can handle it for these girls."

I might have protested that I was happy to do it, but I could tell from the set of her jaw that she desperately wanted to be the one providing that comfort. These women were like her sisters, fellow prisoners who'd come through the same torment she had. I handed over the bag without a word other than, "Of course."

The witch who'd gone to the supply room had brought a few pieces of chalk, so Lesley and I joined Caroline in marking the floor around the second dorm room. As Thalia continued her magicking of the space, the three of us relative intruders retreated to the lounge room where I'd helped encourage the circle of recovering witches before.

Stepping into that familiar space, my gut twinged. How much was this threat going to set back their recovery? They'd been starting to move past the horrors of their experiences, and the demon's approach had brought all that pain back again.

"How close is it?" Lesley asked, looking to me. "Do you know?"

I shook my head. "Not exactly. Lady Northcott didn't think it could reach the edge of the city until sometime tonight." Of course, the demon could start moving faster. I decided not to point out that fact. We had enough to be depressed about as it was.

"That far away, and it's affecting them this much..." Caroline shuddered.

"It's horrible," I said. "It just... doesn't belong here. I can't imagine how easily you must start to sense those energies once you've been exposed to them over and over."

"I still can't believe—" Lesley cut herself off and swiped her mousey bangs away from her face. "I've only been able to find out a little. Everyone's too busy to tell me much. But it sounds like my father got sucked into this 'faction' just a few years ago. I don't even know why. What mattered to them enough that he'd decide it was worth doing that to me? It could be me freaking out with them right now if I'd given in to his pressure."

"I'm sorry," Caroline mumbled. "If I'd had any idea *this* was what my parents were involved in... If I'd stood up to them earlier..."

"It's not your fault," I broke in. "It's theirs. They made the choices. They hurt all those witches for their own gain, and they got very good at hiding it. My father was part of it from before I was born, and I didn't realize until I was almost twenty-five."

If I hadn't, *I* could have been one of these disturbed witches right now. Queasiness bubbled in my stomach.

"Maybe we shouldn't be calling the demons evil," Lesley said. "They don't have any reason to be kind to us. They're like... like wild animals, following their natures. We're supposed to be a community, and look at what we do to ourselves."

She looked so exhausted that I touched her arm. "Not all of us. Not even most of us. Those who committed those crimes will see justice when this is over."

She nodded, but she didn't seem all that comforted. Maybe because we all knew there was no telling when this catastrophe would be over—or whether any of us would survive it.

A thump sounded from the room Thalia was in, followed by a cry. The three of us dashed back to the doorway.

Crystal's cot was tipped on its side. The young witch was clinging to Thalia's arms, tears trickling down her face.

"The gate," she said in a strained whisper. "They're pushing at the gate. They want out—all of them. They're trying to scrape their way through to come here."

Thalia's panicked gaze meet mine. "She was the last one the demons fed on," she said quietly.

The one with the rawest wounds. My throat tightened.

"Do you think it's true?" I asked, and Thalia shook her head, not in denial but in confusion. I stepped closer to the two of them, resting a tentative hand on Crystal's shoulder. "Crystal, what do you feel?"

"I can feel it," she said shakily. "The one that's coming closer. And it can feel them. There's so many of them, behind that doorway in the Cliff. So many of them. And they know now that there's a way to break free."

CHAPTER NINETEEN

Rose

My footsteps clattered down the hall toward the meeting room. I didn't have the wherewithal to try to walk more conscientiously, not with the possibilities whirling through my head.

"Rose?"

I turned to see Gabriel down the hall. He strode to meet me, his eyes dark with concern. "What's wrong? I saw you go by—you look like you've got a wolf at your heels."

More like a demon. I swallowed a burst of hysterical laughter. "The witches the faction used are sensing things from the demon. Things the Assembly *really* needs to know about. I'm about to crash one of their meetings so they do."

"Do you want back-up?" he asked, without a

second's hesitation. Despite my panic, my spark flickered with pleasure at his support.

"It can't hurt," I said. Whatever the Assembly officials thought of me, they thought it whether or not they could see any of my consorts immediately on hand.

I motioned for Gabriel to follow me, and we hurried the rest of the way to the room number I'd gotten after badgering the Northcotts' secretary. I didn't have much space in me for frustration right now, but I couldn't say it didn't irk me that less than an hour after I'd come to Lady Northcott offering even more help than I could have managed before, she'd gone off with who knew how many other officials to discuss strategy without me.

I didn't regret that I'd been able to soothe the recovering witches a little while I was down there, but did she really think I'd have been some kind of hinderance to this discussion rather than an asset?

As I reached the door to the meeting room, I swallowed down that irritation. Without breaking my stride, I shoved inside.

Faces all around the table looked up. It wasn't just the usual bunch—the Northcotts, Remington, Brimsey, Travers, and the head of Defense now that her underling Townsend was being held for questioning—but also a handful of other officials I hadn't met, at least not recently, and a couple other enforcers alongside Ruiz stationed by the walls. Quite a crowd that had shut out me and my consorts and whatever contributions we might have made.

Well, I was here now.

"Lady Hallowell!" Brimsey said sharply, jerking to his feet.

Before he could chide me for rudeness or whatever else was on his mind, I blurted out my horrible news.

"We have to close the portal. Any way we can—it has to be completely sealed, or destroyed—preferably both."

"What are you talking about?" Mr. Northcott said before I could finish.

I spun to face him and his consort. "The witches the faction used can sense the demon's presence even from this distance. And they can sense other things from it too. One of them feels that the other demons are working at breaking through whatever barrier the Frankfords had set up over the portal. No one's been strengthening it. If we just leave it, they'll tear through, and then we'll have dozens of demons to fend off, not just one."

Several faces around the table blanched. Lady Northcott paled too, but she managed to keep her voice steady. "That is alarming news, but we can't act hastily. The barrier has held so far. We have the demon already out to contend with."

"We don't have time to talk about it," I said. "We have no idea how close they might already be."

Brimsey was still standing. "Lady Hallowell," he said, his voice lower but still barbed. "This is a meeting of the highest figures in the Assembly. You can't simply burst in and dictate what the rest of us do."

I couldn't help glowering at him. "I'm sorry I didn't knock and ask permission before shouting, 'Fire!' It's an emergency. It'd be irresponsible for me not to convey just how urgent the situation is."

"You don't know what the actual urgency is," a witch farther down the table said. "And you clearly don't understand all the implications. We—"

Oh, Spark help me. "The *implications?*" I said. "What about the implications of a hundred or more demons crashing into our world? No one here can really be delusional enough to think that we can deal with that kind of assault when we still haven't managed to contain the *one* that's already out."

"Lady Hallowell," Mr. Northcott said. "We appreciate your concern and your call for haste. Let us at least discuss the matter and consider its feasibility."

"Exactly!" the woman who'd mentioned implications piped up. "If you understand the situation fully, the truth is it isn't feasible at all."

Frustration jabbed through me, making my hands clench. "Fine," I said. "If you don't want to do anything about the problem other than talk, I'll see what I can do on my own."

I meant to whirl around and stalk out of there, but I'd barely moved my feet when something hard and narrow smacked into the back of my ribs. A crackling blast of magic flooded me, searing through all my nerves. My skin numbed; my muscles slackened. My legs collapsed under me.

Gabriel caught me before my head would have hit the floor. I could barely hold it up with the way my nerves were still jittering all through my body. I couldn't move my feet to try to pull them back under me.

Nearly everyone around the table had sprung to their feet now. The Northcotts were staring at the figure behind me—an enforcer with his baton clutched in his white-knuckled hand. That was what had hit me: his magicked baton.

"What are you *doing*?" Lady Northcott burst out.

The guard's face had gone blotchy, pale and flushed at the same time. "The way she was talking—the way she came in here—*some*one had to stop her. She's got the demon's power in her, doesn't she? Bringing these men who aren't even witching into our Assembly space. We can't trust her."

I might have been gratified by the horror on the expressions all around me if I hadn't been so shaken from his blow. Gabriel's arm tightened around my back, but I barely felt the contact. My legs still refused to move. My mind swam and steadied, swam and steadied.

"You do *not* act beyond your orders," Mr. Northcott bit out. "That includes striking down a member of our society when no one was in any immediate harm."

"But I—she's a blight on this building since she got here," the enforcer protested.

Lady Northcott flicked her hand, and Investigator Ruiz moved to grab the guy by the arm. He started to pull away, and she made a twisting gesture with her fingers that stilled him in an instant. His baton dropped to the floor.

I tried to say something, but my lips only twitched. A wordless sound escaped me instead. Lady Northcott turned to me, her expression pained.

"I'm so sorry," she said, and for once I thought she really meant it. "He'll be dealt with. We'll do what we can about the portal—I swear it." Her gaze rose to

Gabriel. "With the magicking on those batons, Lady Hallowell won't be able to do very much for an hour or so. She should be given space to recover. Do you need help bringing her to your rooms?"

"No," Gabriel said evenly, but there was a tautness to his voice that told me he was furious under the calm front he was presenting. "I can manage."

He slid his other arm under my knees and scooped me up, tipping me against his chest with my head on his shoulder. I leaned into him as well as I could in an effort to make myself easy cargo.

"As soon as the effects have worn off, reach out to us," Lady Northcott said to me. "We'll talk."

Heat flooded my face at the thought of all those officials watching me be carried out of the room like a helpless child, but I was just glad when the door closed behind us.

Talk. It was all talk. Were they even going to do anything about the portal other than that? But I couldn't express any of that to Gabriel. I just nestled closer, my forehead coming to rest on the side of his neck. He bowed his head as he marched down the hall.

"I've got you," he said. "They're not touching you again. Unless..." He hesitated at the stairs. "If you want me to ask them to send a medic...?"

I managed to rouse my tongue enough to form one word. "No."

His embrace around me tightened. He shouldered aside the door and headed down to the floor below.

The door to our office was open. As Gabriel strode past it to the room with the cots, Kyler and Damon emerged. I guessed Seth and Jin had left to see about the cage like Seth had suggested.

"What happened?" Damon asked, bursting in after us. Anger already burned in his eyes as he watched Gabriel lay me down on the cot.

"One of the enforcers stunned her with his baton," Gabriel said. "Lady Northcott said it'll take about an hour before she can move normally again."

"Fucking hell. The bastards." Damon dropped down beside me, clasping my hand. The heat of his touch coursed through me. My fingers trembled and closed around his, just slightly. A little more sensation, a little more control, seeping back in.

"What can we do?" Ky asked, crouching at my other side and glancing up at Gabriel.

"I don't know," Gabriel said. "It sounded like it'll just wear off on its own. I don't think there's much we *can* do."

He didn't move, though. None of them wanted to leave me. I squeezed Damon's fingers harder. My tongue formed another word that only required the slightest movement of my lips: "Stay."

"Of course, angel," Damon said. "Whatever you need."

"What even happened?" Ky stroked his hand over my hair. "I thought she was down with the witches from the faction. Where did an enforcer come from?"

"One of the witches down there thinks the other demons will break through the portal soon," Gabriel said. "Rose believes her. She went to tell all those Assembly people that we need to shut down the portal, destroy it, but all they did was argue, as usual. The enforcer got pissed off that we hadn't gotten an invitation before coming in."

"Assholes," Damon muttered. "Are you sure we can't just leave them all to be demon food?"

I made a noise of protest, and his expression softened. He kissed the back of my hand, his eyes tender when they met mine. "You know I don't really mean that. I mean, I might like the idea, but I know that's not what we're doing."

Ky leaned in to brush his lips against my cheek and pushed back onto his feet. "I'll see if I can find out what's going on. I've read a fair bit about the portal in the records. If we can convince them to act right away, I should be able to help strategize. Unless you want us all to stay, Rose."

"No," I said, clearer now. "Do... what you can."

He nodded briskly, his mouth twisting at my halting voice, and headed out. He tugged the door shut behind him to protect me from passing glances.

Damon eased me over and climbed onto the cot beside me, pulling me flush against him from chin to feet. "Is this okay, angel?"

"Good," I murmured. My nerves were tingling again, the numbness seeping away. I managed to shift my arm to ease it around his back before the muscles released again. "Better." My body tipped a little farther into his, my core coming to rest against his groin, and a flare of a different sensation shot through me. Hunger. Desire. It burned away some of that horrible helpless feeling.

I wasn't completely helpless. I could ask for what I wanted, and trust the guys with me to offer nothing less.

My jaw clenched up for a second before I worked the next words out. "More. It helps."

Damon tipped his head to meet my eyes, so close his nose grazed mine. I wet my lips, and my fingers traced gentle lines across his back. "What kind of more are you asking for?" he said, his voice gone husky.

I could shift my hips just enough to press against his groin, where he was already hardening. "Rose," Damon murmured.

His lips found mine. He kissed me with more care than usual, as if he were afraid he might break me if he gave his hunger free rein. I found that was exactly what I needed. The warmth of his mouth washed over my skin, and the numbness ebbed even more. His hand eased up under my shirt, and I offered an encouraging noise.

Another hand came to rest on my hip. "How much more do you need?" Gabriel asked, so low the words sent an eager shiver through me.

"Yes, please," I said, and he chuckled.

He lowered himself onto the cot behind me, just fitting onto the edge. Damon shot him a brief look, his eyelids hooded, but then something in him seemed to relax.

"Our consort," he said, still watching Gabriel's expression. There was a note of challenge in his tone, but only faintly.

"Our consort," Gabriel agreed steadily. "To cherish and protect. Together."

The corner of Damon's mouth quirked upward. "We've always been better together, haven't we?"

He dipped his head to kiss a path down my neck. Gabriel ran his hand over my thighs. Enveloped by their bodies, mine was flooded with heat of the best kind. If this was the fastest way through the effects of the baton, at least I could enjoy it while it lasted.

For all I knew, this might be the last moment we had before the end.

CHAPTER TWENTY

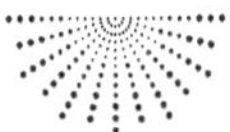

Kyler

hen I made it to the meeting room, the Northcotts were already leaving, other officials trickling out behind them. My feet jarred on the linoleum floor.

"Wait," I said. "Have you come up with a plan for closing the portal already?"

Justin Brimsey, who'd just emerged from the room, crossed his arms over his burly chest. "I don't think that matter should be your concern."

"Of course it's my concern," I said. "That thing is coming this way, isn't it? The other demons might too, if they all get out."

A middle-aged woman with short fawn-brown hair came to a stop in the hall. "We can't worry about the portal right now," she said. "Believe me, we're tackling this in the best way we know how."

"Which is what?" I demanded. "I'm sorry, but you don't have the best track record when it comes to handling problems in a way that actually gets them solved."

"And you think you know better?" Brimsey asked with arched eyebrows.

I raised my chin. "Maybe I do. I've spent the last month going over those records from the Frankfords. I've got to know them better than anyone here does. I don't think it'd necessarily be that difficult to close off the portal, based on the comments about how it was opened in the first—"

"Which will be wonderful, when we're in a position to do that," the woman I didn't know said. "But we're not. So leave it."

"Why the hell not?" I asked. "It wouldn't even have to take that much manpower. I can think of a couple ways—"

Lady Northcott held up her hand. "I know you're Lady Hallowell's consort, and I respect that, but you need to respect our position here too. We know details beyond those records. Do you think we want a catastrophe any more than you do?"

"Of course not," I said. "But ignoring this doesn't make any sense. When you look at the facts—"

Brimsey sighed and meandered off in the other direction as if the argument was boring him. I bristled, but at the same time I took in the expressions on the faces of the officials still facing me. Defensive, resistant. Just like I was feeling.

Well, how did they expect me to act when they were

ignoring all the research I'd done, all the knowledge I could share, just out of hand?

That thought drew me up short. It was hard not to think of Jin just an hour ago, laying into us for getting stuck in the same old patterns. Telling us to try new angles, step outside what was comfortable.

What if the point here wasn't all the things I did know that they were dismissing, but the things I didn't know? Because, if I was being honest, there were probably an awful lot of the latter. This wasn't my world, no matter how much research material I'd gotten my hands on. I'd only been a part of it, and only in a small way, for a few months.

I took a deep breath and ignored the balking sensation in my chest. I was supposed to be the guy with the answers, the guy the others could count on to know or find the key info that they needed. But going all know-it-all with the Assembly hadn't gotten me anywhere in the last few days. I could admit the gaps in my knowledge too, couldn't I?

"I'm sorry," I said, slower and more evenly than before. "I rushed in, and I don't have the full picture. It was wrong for me to act as if I did. There's obviously a lot I don't understand about the situation. But I want to understand—I want to be in a position to help later if I can. Is there time for someone to explain to me what the issues with closing the portal are?"

"So you can shoot them all down the second you get the gist of them?" Lady Northcott said skeptically.

My face flushed. That was sort of what I'd already

been doing. "I swear I'll listen with an open mind. And mouth zipped." I drew my thumb across my lips.

Mr. Northcott's mouth twitched into something that was almost a smile. He glanced at the woman who'd spoken up earlier. "What do you say, Lady Paulson? Did you have any urgent business on your side of things?"

"No," the woman said, but with a certain amount of hesitation. The way she looked at me was skeptical too.

"Please," I said. "All I want to do is help, however I can. I was coming at it badly. But I can't do anything at all if I don't have all the necessary context. And if you know more about the portal than is in those records... I'm kind of dying to understand this whole situation better, to be honest."

Lady Paulson's jaw worked. "All right," she said, not sounding all that happy with her decision. "Come on. I want to be in my office if any new reports arrive."

With that underwhelming welcome, I couldn't say I was all that enthusiastic about the short hike across the building and down to a little office about the same size as the one I'd spent most of the last few days working in. Inside, maps, a large one of the state and several smaller ones with more detail of specific counties, hung on the wall beside a neatly organized desk. A broad whiteboard gleamed on the far wall, the lingering scent of the markers making my nose twitch.

Lady Paulson strode right up to the desk and grabbed a folder off the top of a pile. "You want to understand?" she said. "It's all here. People I work with have been out in the field observing this creature and the gateway it emerged through from the first moment we knew about the Cliff. Testing them with magic. Collecting every observation they could possibly make."

"And?" I said, and caught myself before I could point out all the things I already knew. "What have you seen that makes you think the rest of the demons aren't a threat?"

"Oh, they are," Paulson said. "They're just not as great a threat as what will happen if we manage to close the portal while the demon already out is still on the loose."

I blinked at her. "Okay. I think you're going to have to lay that out for me step by step."

She sighed. "You haven't been close to this thing, have you? What has your consort told you about the impression it gives her?"

Rose's comments from the few times she'd encountered the demon came back to me easily. "It feels unnatural. Like there's something just *wrong* about it, some kind of dissonance in the energy it gives off. Just being near it makes her queasy."

Paulson nodded. "We don't understand very much about the realm these creatures come from, but it's clearly not one that can exist in harmony with our own. The witches who've gone out to study the portal and the Cliff around it, as well as those who've been tracking the creature that escaped, have experimented with various sorts of magic and tested the destruction it leaves behind. None of *our* innate energy has the effect we'd expect."

"That's why Rose has been so important to the efforts to stop it," I said. This was all information I already knew, but I reined in my impatience. "Because she has a little of the demon-type energy in her magic."

"Yes. But the other consequence..." Paulson paused and contemplated me. "With all the reading you've done, what do you think would happen if we managed to kill this creature?"

What kind of question was that? "Well, I guess you'd... bury it somewhere?" I said. "Or burn the body? And then we'd be done with it."

She gave me a crooked smile. "That would work if the demon were a creature of this realm. But as Lady Hallowell has noted, it doesn't correspond with this world at all. The effects we would expect from an ordinary beast don't apply."

"Which means...?"

"One of the initial attempts to stop the demon resulted in a small fragment of its... well, let's just say *skin*... being sliced off. The witch who managed that, it immediately killed." Paulson gave me a pointed look as if to say I shouldn't try the same myself and then opened up the folder to a photograph. A ragged bit of dark gray material with a reddish glow around the edges lay on a white surface.

"Dead flesh," she went on. "As it were. But it would not burn away and it showed no signs of rotting. What it *did* do is deteriorate any surface it was placed on for more than a few minutes. It seared holes in that table. We couldn't find any material of this world that could consistently contain it."

The bottom dropped out of my stomach. If a tiny piece of the demon did that, then what effect would an entire immense corpse have? "What did you do with it?" I asked.

"We ran all the experiments we could, moving it often, and then when we'd exhausted the possibilities we could think of and didn't want to see any more equipment damaged, we tossed it back through the portal." She closed the folder and glanced up at me. "Which is what we need to do with that demon, alive or dead, once we manage to contain it."

"And if we close up the portal while it's still here, then we're stuck with it—and whatever ways it'll keep destroying this world even if it's dead."

"Yes." Her lips formed a tight smile. "So you see, our primary focus has to be getting the one demon back to its proper home as quickly as possible. Only then can we focus on sealing its gateway into this world."

The explanation made sense. I hadn't seen any hint of this possibility in the Frankfords' records—but then, how could they have known? They'd never let any of the demons through to see what effect they might have on this world.

I swallowed my nausea. "I'm sorry I was so pushy before. If you'd told us—told Rose—"

Paulson lowered her head. "It isn't information the higher officials want spread through the entire witching community. That would cause even more panic. We couldn't discuss it openly in front of everyone at that meeting. But—maybe I should have made more of an effort to speak with Lady Hallowell about it, to take her aside. I was startled when she burst in, and, well..."

"You don't think all that highly of her or us," I

finished for her, without much rancor. "We've noticed that's the general attitude. It's kind of hard to miss."

"You do want to contribute, though, don't you?" She peered at me curiously. "You had no idea magic even existed until recently, from what I understand? Lady Hallowell has said she didn't reveal that secret until shortly before your consorting."

"That's true," I said. "But I didn't have to see that much to believe in it. It's hard to deny something that's happening right in front of you. Honestly, all I want is to learn as much as I can so that I can really contribute. I'm pretty good at putting pieces together and finding possible answers... if I have all the pieces to start with."

"And you have had access to the Frankfords' files for weeks longer than we have." Paulson hesitated, and then said, "You've requested access to the full Assembly server. There are some sections that must stay secure—I don't have authority over them in the first place. But I can't see any reason you shouldn't be able to look through our general records and historical archives, in case that gives you a better grounding, more context for what you've read already."

My heart lifted. "Really? That would be amazing. Now?"

A warmer smile touched her face at my enthusiasm. "I can set you up. But first—can you swear that any insights you gain, you'll share with the Assembly rather than the bunch of you running off on your own?"

Her hand twitched as she spoke, and the air vibrated around us. I had the sense that my answer was going to be binding in a literal way. But that was all right. She'd trusted me—I could return that favor.

"I swear I'll consult with Assembly officials before we take any action," I said.

"All right. Then let's get you started."

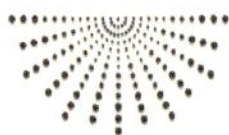

CHAPTER TWENTY-ONE

Rose

Walking into the Assembly's holding building wasn't any more fun than it had been on my previous trip. I rubbed my arms as I stared down the dull gray hall, the faint chemical smell in the air trickling into my lungs. The afternoon had turned overcast, heavy clouds congealing in the sky, but the air conditioning in here was still at full blast.

I pushed myself onward. Coming here had been my idea, but I didn't want to spend any more time in this place than I had to. Investigator Ruiz, my sole companion this time, kept pace with me, our shoes tapping against the tiled floor.

"I have approval to use further truth compulsion, if you think it's necessary," she said. "You're not to cast that sort of magic yourself."

"I know," I said. "I don't think it'll really help us with

the sort of information I'm hoping to get today. But if I think one of them is hiding something we can only get that way, I'll let you know."

Starting things off with a truth spell made the conversation automatically twice as antagonistic. Not that I was feeling especially friendly toward the two men I might speak to today, but we'd already gotten the straight-forward facts from them. I wanted impressions, insights, the sorts of things it was easy to weasel around saying under compulsion, if they decided to. By going in with good faith, maybe I'd earn a little in return.

Or maybe they could just give enough of a damn about the rest of us to want to make sure the demon didn't raze this city to the ground.

Ruiz motioned to indicate which door led to Charles Frankford's holding cell. He and his wife, Helen, had led their faction together for decades, but I had the feeling he was the one more invested. He'd been the one gaining a sort of magic from it. He'd been the one who'd gone to the greatest lengths to stop me from uncovering their conspiracy.

I doubted there was anyone in the world who had greater experience with demonkind than he did.

Ruiz unlocked the door. The air in the room inside was a little warmer, but I had to suppress a shiver anyway, stepping inside to face the man who'd orchestrated so many horrors.

Frankford leaned back against the wall at the sight of me, his expression tensing in defiance even though he was looking a little haggard. The Justice division didn't believe in torture, but I remembered what it had been like trapped in one of these little rooms for just half a day. The boredom would be eating at him, along with the restriction of movement. He was probably stewing over the possible sanctions he'd face when the current emergency was over and he could be brought to proper trial.

I wasn't sure I could hope any guilt had come into that mix, as much as it would have been deserved.

"Lady Hallowell," he said, his voice crisp if a little hoarse.

"Mr. Frankford. I thought we should talk a little more."

"About what? I've talked to plenty of people since I've been brought in here. I'm not sure there's any thought in my head that hasn't been overturned and examined."

He sounded almost sulky about it. I caught myself on the verge of gritting my teeth. As if it wasn't justice for him to be here after everything he'd done. But I couldn't let my temper get the better of me.

"You know the demon is making its way toward the city," I said. "It looks as though it'll reach the outskirts overnight."

"Not my doing," he replied flatly. "I was perfectly content to have them stay on the other side of that portal."

"It's your family who opened that portal in the first place," I couldn't help retorting. "You maintained it all this time. The fiends wouldn't have had the chance if it wasn't for you."

He shrugged. "Did you come to tell me things I already know, girl?"

The dismissive label annoyed me almost as much as his careless attitude did. I dragged in a breath. "I'm here because you *have* been involved for so long. You've seen more of the demons than anyone else. I'm sure you've been forced to share every fact about them you've discovered. But there's got to be more than that—things you couldn't prove, ideas, suspicions. Anything your instincts told you that you never completely confirmed. We need everything we can get, even if it's a longshot. Would you please help us stop it before it shatters this city and possibly all of us in it?"

Any emotion that had been in his eyes before had drained away. "My life is already over. Because of you. I've told the Assembly everything I know that could help. I'm not going to speculate wildly so that I can be blamed for further catastrophes."

"That's not—"

He turned his face away, his body rigid, and I knew I wasn't getting anything else from him. Maybe there really wasn't anything else. Ideas so shaky they led us in the wrong direction weren't going to fix this mess.

"Mr. Frankford," Ruiz said. "I'll just remind you that Lady Hallowell is here by the authority of the Northcotts, and a rejection of her request is a rejection of them."

"I'm not rejecting," he said, sounding only tired now. "I have nothing to offer."

The enforcer glanced at me. I shook my head, my mouth tight. We couldn't have dragged vague suppositions out of him with any magic, even if I'd been sure he had something more than might be useful.

My legs balked for a second when Ruiz had shut the door behind us. My gaze found the other room on my agenda without any guidance.

If Frankford had given us something useful, I could have skipped the second visit. But he hadn't. I didn't know whether my chances were better with my second option or worse. Maybe a little of both in different ways.

"Ready?" Ruiz asked, a hint of sympathy in her tone.

"As much as I'm going to be."

She opened the door to my father's room. He sat up at the swing of its opening, his expression almost hopeful until he caught sight of me. His face—his whole body, really—went still.

We didn't have to exchange a single word for me to be able to tell that he knew I was now aware of the full extent of his crimes against me. He had to have realized I'd find out after the interrogators had forced the information out of him.

For almost twenty-five years of my life, I'd known that face better than any other. Now I could hardly stand to look at it. The idea of calling him "Dad" out loud, as if nothing had changed, made my throat constrict.

"Mr. Hallowell, Lady Hallowell has requested an interview with you," Ruiz said, breaking the silence. "She comes with full authority from the Assembly."

Dad eyed me warily. "What do you want to ask me about now?" he said, his voice almost creaky. There was a hesitation in it, as if he wasn't totally sure he wanted me to answer.

Did he think I'd come in here to hash out my personal complaints? Every time I spoke with him, I was reminded more and more of how little he must really have thought of me.

"The demon has almost reached the city," I said. "We need to understand everything about it that we can. You've been involved with this faction... for a long time." At least the entirety of my life, and presumably a fair number of years before. "You've had their power in you. You've been there for the rituals to use and bind them. If there are any impressions, even vague ones, that you didn't share with the previous interrogators because you weren't sure they were important, I want to hear them now."

"Impressions," he repeated dully.

"About the demons. How they behave. What affects them. What they're drawn to or repelled by. Even if it was nothing but a hint and you're only speculating." I paused and forced out the last word. "Please."

His gaze had dropped as I'd spoken, but it jerked back to my face at the plea. For a few seconds I thought he was going to refuse like Frankford had. Then he let out a ragged breath, his eyes going distant.

"I'm not sure there's anything I haven't already talked about," he said. "I never delved too deeply into the logistics—I never wanted to. And we couldn't see much of their behavior through the portal. We only knew as much as we did by how they responded to what we offered them. And we never offered more than the usual, while I was there."

"The usual," I prompted, even though I knew what

he meant. The more he talked, the more likely something useful would come out.

He grimaced. "The creatures seemed to crave something about our essence. We've been over that. Taking magic from a witch appeared to sate them for a while, enough that Frankford could control them somewhat…" His forehead furrowed. "I remember thinking it was almost as if they got drunk on it, unable to reason clearly, and that was why he could manipulate them then."

Huh. I hadn't heard any of the faction members describe it like that before, but I couldn't say the insight helped any. A drunken demon lumbering around the city sounded even worse than a sober one.

"Drunk could also mean more erratic and harder to control," I pointed out.

"Well, maybe. I don't know what they acted like when they moved away from the portal to do whatever they do in that aberrant realm. Occasionally they drifted into what looked like a bit of a stupor, but that wasn't consistent enough that I'd stake anything on it."

A stupor. The word sent me back a few hours to my hurried ministrations with the recovering witches as they'd panicked—sending a cloud of calm down over them. An idea prickled up from the back of my mind. We'd tried shoving the demon back, and we'd tried subtly maneuvering it into a trap, but we hadn't attempted to lull it. There wouldn't have been much point in simply slowing it down temporarily as an effect by itself, but maybe in combination with the other strategies we'd been developing…

"Does that get you anywhere?" Dad asked with apparent curiosity.

I wrenched my thoughts back to the present. I had no interest in discussing my uncertain ideas with him.

"I don't know," I said. "We'll see. Anything else about them, or their power?"

His mouth tightened. "I don't like to think about how it felt, having that energy in me. Like this constant tremor of wrongness I could never completely ignore. But you must know about that at least as well as I ever did."

His tone was prodding. My back stiffened. "I don't think you want to go there with me," I said.

He kept looking at me intently. "It can't have been that bad. You didn't have any idea until I told them. Enough to light up your spark that much more, but not enough to poison it."

"You had no right," I said. "To do that to me—to do that to my mother... You couldn't have known what it would do. You brought a monster's essence to me, let it touch me, before I was even *born*."

My voice was shaking by the last word. I clamped my mouth shut.

"I did know," Dad started to say. "I told them—I wanted to stop him, to stop the whole—"

"Shut. Up," I bit out. "I don't want to hear about it. Your explanations have changed so many times, I can't possibly believe any claim you make. So stop trying to explain. It's never going to be forgivable, no matter what you say."

His expression wavered. "It wasn't all bad, was it?"

he said quietly. "I've seen it in you already—how important your magic is to you. How much it means to you to wield that power. You're the witch you are because of what I gave you, Rose. Everything you're capable of is thanks to that."

"I am *never* going to thank you," I snapped before he could go on. "Don't you dare try to tell me who I am." A quiver ran through my body. I didn't think we were getting any further here—and I wasn't sure I trusted my reactions enough to try. "That's enough."

I spun on my heel and stalked out. Ruiz followed, shutting the door. I didn't want to look at her, didn't want to risk seeing that she agreed with him, even a little.

Even I wasn't totally sure he was wrong. The power I had, the exhilaration of that magic, the awe I'd been able to inspire in others... I couldn't say that hadn't meant anything to me at all.

"What now?" Ruiz asked.

"I think the first part of that conversation might have sparked a little inspiration," I said. "I should talk to the Northcotts and their advisors—and my consorts." Ky would want to be able to share his perspective based on his research, certainly. I headed toward the main doors. "We'll need to confirm the status of the cage reconstruction, and—"

A figure in enforcer clothes burst into the hall, her gaze wild as it search the hall and snagged on us. "Lady Hallowell," she said. "Investigator Ruiz. Your presence is requested right away. The demon has sped up its approach. At its current pace—it could be at the edge of the city within the hour."

CHAPTER TWENTY-TWO

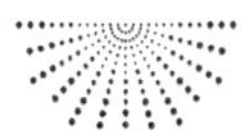

Rose

When we made it to the main Assembly building, it looked as if the entire staff was flooding out under the thickly clouded sky. Enforcers were scrambling into the cars parked along the road, and more vehicles were pouring from the underground parking garage. Ruiz's hand clamped around my arm as a humid wind whipped through our hair.

"Come on," she said. "There's no time for meetings now. Whatever ideas you have, you'll have to share them over the phone while we head out to intercept it."

A breathless minute later, I found myself crammed in the back seat of a small sedan with two enforcers, another at the wheel and Ruiz beside him. The car's wheels squealed against the pavement as we swayed around the bend. The growl of the engine sounded nearly as anxious as my thudding heart.

"Do you know anything else about what's going on?" I asked the other enforcers. "What's the demon doing? Has it hurt anyone else?"

"We just got the report to move out," the woman next to me said. "From what I heard, it's been picking up speed for the last several minutes without any signs of slowing down. I didn't hear any new casualties reported, but if it reaches the fringes..."

She didn't need to finish that sentence. My fingers curled around the door handle as if it could provide some comfort. "No one has any idea what changed—why it's in a hurry now?"

The enforcer shook her head. "Not that I've heard about."

"I've got Lady Northcott on the line," Ruiz said. She swiveled in her seat to hold out her phone to me. "Fill her in on whatever your thinking, and if she agrees she can get started on coordinating."

"Thanks." My lungs were tight as I accepted the phone. "Lady Northcott—hello."

The head of the Assembly's measured voice filtered through the speaker. "Lady Hallowell. Please tell me this idea of yours is something we can implement immediately."

I choked on a desperate laugh. "Maybe. Let's see what you think of the plan first."

* * *

We didn't witness any sign of panic until we reached the suburbs. A minivan came racing past us on the opposite side of the freeway, the driver weaving erratically from lane to lane to gain every bit of distance she could. One glimpse of her pale face made my stomach sink.

She'd seen the demon. I had no doubt about that. And recently enough that she was still in flight mode.

The closer we got to the edge of the city, the more speeding vehicles zoomed past in the opposite direction. Where the streets on either side of the freeway started to give way to wilder land, a blockade had been set up on our side. The hum of magic in the air told me those police officers were only enforcers in costume. They were keeping as many people as possible away from the site of the demon's impending arrival.

The officers waved our vehicles through while turning back everyone else. The driver put his foot down on the gas pedal as soon as we were passed in on the less crowded stretch beyond. We flew across the asphalt and skidded around the exit ramp to reach the smaller road where we were going to make our stand.

If the demon didn't change directions as well as pace in the next several minutes, that was.

The terrain looked like as good a spot as any for an ambush on this short notice. We parked at an overgrown field, a sign at the edge announcing that it would be built up into a little townhouse development sometime next year. A familiar truck was already stationed partway into the long grass, where workers were moving around the sprawled bars of the refurbished cage. I spotted Seth's brawny form and Jin's leaner one next to him, and my pulse hitched.

"Fan out!" the sergeant was shouting near the car she'd arrived in. The enforcers were streaming around her to encircle the field. Our supplies hadn't arrived yet, from the looks of things, but how could I have expected them to? It'd taken a few minutes to walk Lady Northcott through my plan and several more before we'd hashed it out to the point that she'd felt we had something solid—or at least more solid than anything they'd already come up with. The delivery she'd sent would take time to catch up.

"I'm waiting for the magicking materials," I told Ruiz. "I've got to talk to my consorts first."

She gave me an unreadable look and a brisk nod. I realized she'd never really indicated what she thought of my unusual choice of consorts. I supposed she couldn't be too bothered by it, anyway, or some derision would have slipped into her attitude toward me by now. Not everyone was totally caught up in their prejudices.

A distant rumbling crept through the clouds overhead. Another gust of wind tossed my hair as I jogged across the field to where Seth was stalking along the perimeter of the trap. Its base was still set on the truck's flatbed, the flaps dangling around that square.

Seth raised his head at the sound of my footsteps. His eyes brightened, but the smile his mouth formed was grim.

"How close is it?" he asked.

"I don't know," I admitted. The sergeant must have had an idea—she'd be getting reports from the enforcers tracking the thing. From the increasing urgency in her shouts, it clearly wasn't that far off. "Close, I think."

Before I could say anything else, he grasped my shoulder. "I'm staying this time. Some of the walls of the cage still need some work. I'll get as much as I can done as quickly as I can, until it's too late."

An ache filled my chest, but what could I say to him? We did need him here, maybe more than any of the others working on the cage. If I was willing to put myself in the line of fire where I could help, I had to let him take that risk too.

"I get it," I said. "But as soon as it comes close…"

"I won't do anything stupid," he said. He dipped his head for a kiss, fast and hard, and turned back to his work.

"I overheard some of the enforcers talking about some new plan," Jin said, coming up beside me. "They mentioned glyphs. If you could use some extra manpower in the drawing department…?"

I shot him a grateful smile, even though my heart squeezed all over again. He'd never had to face the demon directly before either. Now two of my consorts were going to be coming so close.

But having him working with us could make all the difference.

"Yes," I said. "I'll show you."

I fumbled for something to draw on, and Jin produced a small notepad and a pencil from his pocket. With a few quick strokes, I sketched the glyphs I'd used to cast the calming spell over the recovering witches' dorm rooms.

Jin studied the paper, his finger tracing the lines. "Where do you want them?"

"All around the field," I said. "In a semicircle, so the demon doesn't have to cross any to come inside but it'll be nearly surrounded then. Just alternate between the different glyphs. You can use—" My gaze caught on a truck speeding along the road toward us. "I think the tools I asked for to make breaking the ground easily will be here in less than a minute."

"What's all this do?" my consort asked. "What *is* the plan?"

My stomach twisted before I spoke. It wasn't as brilliant as I'd have liked it to be. It was just the best we had.

"We're going to try to lull it into a daze," I said. "Slow and sleepy. And then when its guard is down, maybe we'll be able to shove it onto the cage so we can trap it before it wakes up enough to really fight back."

"Sounds worth a shot," Jin said.

His arms slipped around my waist in the briefest of embraces, and then the truck screeched to a halt at the side of the road. We rushed over to join the enforcers who'd been assigned prep duty.

Jin grabbed a narrow hoe-like implement to dig the glyphs into the earth and hurried off again. I hefted up a large bag of lavender powder. For people, it had an actual chemical effect as well as its magical properties. I didn't really think the demon would be affected the same way, but hopefully the magical enhancement and our own associations as we worked our magicking would make it a useful addition.

Figures scattered the field, carving glyphs. A few of the other enforces and I spread out between them, scattering lavender powder all around the field except the far end where the demon was approaching.

I was only halfway through my bag when the first nausea-inducing tremor carried through the air. The hairs on the back of my neck rose. "It's close!" someone shouted farther down the field.

I tossed the rest of my powder across the grass as quickly as I could. Then I dashed back to the ring the enforcers had formed, crouched low in the grass. The tall uneven blades tickled my arms as I knelt among them. Their warm scent mingled with the lingering essence of lavender rubbed into my hands. The clouds let out another faint rumble of thunder.

"Here it comes," a witch near me murmured. A second later, I wouldn't have needed her to tell me. The dissonant rippling of energy washed over me even more strongly. I couldn't restrain a shudder.

The hulking glowing form came into view less than a minute later. It barged into the field at such a swift pace compared to the cautious meandering I'd seen before that my pulse stuttered.

The enforcers all around me straightened up at the same moment, and I pushed myself to my feet to join them. To join their spell, weaving peace and calm through the atmosphere and casting it out toward the demon.

A cool airy sensation settled over me as I moved through the form, drowning out some of the demon's energy and the stormy tinge in the atmosphere. Our magic flowed around and past me in a softly soothing wave. All around the edges of the field, the enforcers swept through the same movements, our efforts building on each other.

The demon's gait slowed. Its head drooped and listed to the side. It peered at us with those flat black eyes that chilled me almost as much as its eerie energy did. It kept up its swaying journey across the field, but with each step, it covered less ground. The next step came later, and later.

I spun in a careful circle, my arms lifting and descending beside me, and when I looked at the creature again, it was moving at no more than the shuffle I'd seen when I'd gone to observe it the first time.

It *was* still moving, though. Lurching bit by bit across the field, its gaze intent enough that I didn't have much hope we could toss it into the cage just yet. The grass around its oddly jointed limbs sagged and grayed.

I hadn't really drawn on my demon-tainted power yet, not anywhere near as much as I could. I hadn't been sure how that effect might interact with the spell. But in another ten, maybe fifteen seconds the demon might already be out of range of the trap. Sucking in a breath, I reached down into the depths of my spark to seek out that uneasy thread.

There. I focused on the unpleasant tremor despite the churning of my stomach and threw myself into the form a little faster. If we couldn't lull the demon into a total daze, maybe I could bludgeon it into one. Gently.

I tossed out surge after surge of compulsion—to drag at its limbs, to darken its mind, to numb it almost like I'd been numbed by the enforcer's baton, just all the way down to its thoughts. Whatever thoughts a demon even was capable of.

The fiend leaned forward onto its knuckles and rocked there for a second. My spirits lifted. I whirled again to cast one more burst of that numbing binding around it, almost giddy at the amount of power that was reverberating through me now. *Yes. You will bend to my will. You will—*

The creature jerked around, its head swinging toward me with that blank gaze. My nerves jumped with electric chill. My hands wavered, just for an instant—and in that instant, the demon lunged.

Seth

I'd heard Gabriel and Damon—and Rose, of course—describe what being in a demon's presence was like, more than once. But either they'd downplayed the effect or what they'd said hadn't totally sunk in.

When that massive humanoid form pushed between the trees at the opposite end of the field, my heart seemed to literally rattle against my ribs. For a few seconds, the alarm clanging all through my body stole my ability to even breathe. I could only stare, paralyzed, as the dimly glowing creature clambered in its deformed ape-like way through the tall grass.

"Holy fuck," Jin murmured behind me, sounding choked. His voice woke me up, enough to remember that the plan was to put the demon in a stupor, not to fall into one ourselves.

And after they'd stupefied it, Rose and the enforcers were going to propel it into the cage I was standing right next to. So now might be a good time to move well out of the way.

My legs wobbled as I shifted backward. Jin gripped my elbow, supporting me and seeking support at the same time. When I glanced back, his face had grayed under his tan skin. His mouth was frozen with lips slightly parted in horrified awe.

The demon was still lurching toward us. A bolt of panic raced through me, and my legs finally started working.

Jin stumbled backward with me as I hauled us away from the cage, away from the truck, to the edge of the field where the enforcers were swaying through the motions of their magicking dance. My heart was still thumping painfully hard. I didn't know where Rose was in the wide semi-circle around the field—didn't know whether trying to find her was even a good idea. She hadn't wanted any of us, any of her consorts, out here with her because she'd be distracted worrying about us. I was not about to prove that concern right.

The enforcers stood on their own patches of land, just enough space between them so they could sweep through the motions of their forms without bumping into each other. They'd left no room for anyone to squeeze past them. Jin swiped his hand over his forehead, his gaze starting to clear, and tugged for me to crouch down with him near the inner edge of their ring. The closest we could get to any sort of safety.

"I had no idea—I never really thought—" A hoarse

chuckle slipped out of his mouth. He pressed his knuckles to his lips, his gaze fixing on the demon again. When mine followed his, a fresh surge of horror tore through my nerves.

That *face* so huge and gnarled and yet with features I could identify as human-like. Those darkly opaque eyes that seemed to see nothing and everything at the same time, like twin voids lodged in the creature's deformed skull...

I tensed my muscles against another shudder and wrenched my gaze to the side. I just wouldn't look at it if I couldn't look without my thoughts spiraling away from me. We'd have a lot better chance of surviving if I kept my head.

"Do you think their magic is working?" Jin asked under his breath. "The demon looks like it's slowing down."

Taking note from the corner of my vision, I had to agree. The creature's lumbering pace had faltered. The unsettling vibes that rolled off it jarred against my nerves even harder. I fought to keep my breathing steady. In and out, just like always.

Rose and the other witches had the situation under control. This was their job. I'd done mine. The best thing I could do right now was stay out of their way.

But the thing kept shuffling onward, almost directly toward us. My jaw started to ache from how tightly I'd clamped my teeth together. The demon had slowed down, yeah, but had they dazed it enough? How much of an effect was their spell even having?

A blur of movement, a familiar purple shirt, caught my eye in the curve of the semi-circle around the side of the field. Rose's dark hair fanned out around her pale face as she bowed and reached in a dance of her own. A faster dance than the enforcers were using. I knew, down in the sensation of light that warmed me from the inside out at the sight of her, that she was casting something more potent, drawing on the reserves of magic inside her that were now even greater because of how closely she and the five of us were interlinked.

The demon came to a stop. The grass around it started to curl with rot. Nausea swelled in my gut, but a little hope unfurled alongside it. If anyone could manage this, it was Rose. Was the demon under her spell?

In the space of a heartbeat, it whipped toward her. A shout of warning snagged in my throat. Jin let out a low desperate sound, and the demon barreled forward. Straight at my consort and the witches around her.

The wind warbled, and my bones trembled with it. I shoved myself upright, but then I didn't know what to do with myself. It wasn't as if I could reach Rose before the demon did. It wasn't as if I had any way of fending it off even if I could have made it there.

Rose wasn't standing down. I could tell from her expression that she'd seen the demon charging toward her, but she only adjusted her form, her hands slicing through the air, her legs slashing out. The demon leapt, its claws swiping at the gathered witches, and Rose shoved her arms forward.

Both demon and the enforcers around her pitched

backward and sprawled on the ground. The aftershock of the colliding forces trembled through the ground all the way to my feet.

Rose's shoulders shuddered, but she was already moving again. Magicking again. The other witches milled around her, some of them attempting spells of their own, some of them fleeing toward the cars. The ones near us were dispersing too, to try to help push the demon back or to find shelter.

The demon had righted itself in an instant. It let out a sound somewhere between a groan and a roar and lunged at the witches again.

This time whatever magic Rose was summoning wasn't enough to completely block the fiend's attack. Its vicious claws severed the neck of one woman and gouged others across the shoulders, the belly. Blood painted the grass red.

I took a step forward and stopped myself. "If we die, Rose dies too," I said.

"What the fuck can we do?" Jin said miserably. "We can't just— It's going to slaughter them."

The enforcers' sergeant had clearly realized the same thing. Her shouts for retreat echoed across the field. The demon wheeled at her voice, and for the first time seemed to consider the cars. My heart sank. No, no—

The monster sprang away from its previous victims across the grass. The purposefulness of its movements left no doubt in my mind that it meant to wrench every one of those vehicles apart like it had our cage last time. And then it would plow through all our fragile bodies and Lord only knew how much else of the city we'd been fighting to protect.

We still had the cage—constructed out of copper and imbued with witches' blood and Rose's fierce energy. But the witches couldn't even keep the demon *off* them, let alone shove it all the way over—

The thought clicked into place in my head with a sudden certainty. I'd just have to bring the cage to it.

I was already running to the truck. "Seth!" Jin called, but I didn't hesitate. My thoughts spun in my head—I had to consider the possibilities, evaluate the risk—what if I hurt more people than I helped racing in there?

But there was no time for that. There was only the demon loping across the field toward our only means of escape, barely stumbling when another wave of magic hit it, and damn it, if I didn't do *something* I was going to spend the rest of my life, however short it might be, hating myself for it.

I jumped into the cab of the truck. The key was sitting on the dashboard. I shoved it into the ignition, jerked the controls into reverse, and hit the gas with a slam of my foot.

The truck lurched backwards with a roar to rival the demon's. The walls of the cage that had been leaning against the ground pulled off the hinges we'd left open for the final sealing. The base, lying on the truck's flatbed, rattled but held in place.

The truck quaked but kept moving, picking up speed even over the bumpy terrain. My foot jammed on the gas pedal, I craned my neck and yanked the steering wheel I was clutching, aiming the panel behind me directly into the demon's path.

The demon loomed, my nerves screamed, and the truck's wheels jolted beneath me. Then the slab of glyph-twisted metal and magic collided with that monstrous form.

The demon's torso smacked the copper shapes I'd formed so carefully. It screeched and heaved itself away. Its arm lashed out.

A surge of nerve-rattling power blasted into the cabin and threw me right through the windshield. I barely managed to wrench my wobbling arms across my face to shield myself from the spray of shattered glass. My back hit the hood, a knife of agony stabbing up and down my spine. Heat seared my skin.

"Come on!" someone was hollering, and someone else screamed, and the rest of the world narrowed down to the throbbing in my back and the stinging of my skin, and God help me, I wanted to peel it right off of my flesh, or—

Hands caught me, hauling me off the hood of the truck. Something clattered to my right. I was hefted between two bodies that I had the vague impression were much too slight to really be able to carry me. *Magic*, I thought dazedly, and then, *Rose.*

They were pulling me away from her. They were—

I wasn't sure how much I even managed to move. I must have at least flailed a bit. One of my rescuers cursed, and the other did something that froze my limbs in place with a chill that wasn't entirely unpleasant. And then Rose's voice was there, only a foot or two from my ear, quavering with panic but present. That was all I could have asked for.

"Will he be okay?" she said. "Is he—"

As if my mind had been holding on just to confirm her presence, I never got to hear the rest of that sentence. The world tumbled away from me completely.

CHAPTER TWENTY-FOUR

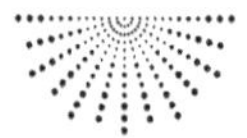

Rose

"Seth? Can you hear me yet?" I rested my trembling hand against my consort's cheek, the gentle strokes of my fingers willing more magic from me to him.

We'd been tearing down the road for a couple of minutes now, and he still hadn't woken up. With each passing second, my heart thumped harder with the worry that he might never wake up at all.

The enforcers who'd grabbed Seth off the hood of the truck had carried him to the nearest vehicle: the minivan that had arrived with our extra supplies. We were tucked into the middle seat, the air around us tart with the scent of lavender, three enforcers in the back and two up front. The wheels shuddered over the pot-holed surface as the engine roared at speeds this road was never meant to endure.

Seth's brawny body sprawled awkwardly in the tight space, one leg on the verge of sliding off the seat. I had his head and shoulders on my lap, a reversal of the pose I'd found myself in after my last encounter with the demon. Except then I'd passed out from overextending myself. Seth had been caught head-on in a blast of demonic energy. I didn't even know how much damage he might have taken.

I was healing every injury I could see: the scorched-gray streaks on his arms and where the unnatural magic had burned through his clothes, the cuts where shards of broken glass had sliced into his skin. But I didn't know how to stir him out of unconsciousness, or if I should even try to. None of the enforcers who'd leapt into the van with us in our hasty escape had more than the standard first aid training.

Engines were rumbling all around us. Horns blared as we careened onto the main road toward the city. Was the blockade still up on the freeway to stop people from heading this way? Did it even matter?

The demon's hollow roar carried over the landscape behind us. There was a thunderous thud and a smash like crumpling steel. My stomach flipped with the certainty that it had caught one of our cars and dashed it against the ground with all its monstrous strength.

"Where the fuck are we going to go?" one of the enforcers up front was saying. "We can't stop that thing."

"We regroup at the Assembly building. That's the plan," the other said.

"And *then* what?"

"I don't know. There's got to be something."

There's got to be something. I traced my fingertips over Seth's slack face again, fighting to focus on the healing magic I was offering him and not the turmoil of emotion inside me. I didn't even know where Jin was—I hadn't seen him in the final chaos.

He had to be alive. I wouldn't be if he wasn't. The connection between us still shone through my veins, and without the pained flicker of my bond with Seth. But I had no idea how close the demon might be on his heels. The cries and the thunder of its approach seemed to be getting louder.

A tree blackened and torn up by the roots hurtled past us to crash by the side of the road. The driver swerved, just barely avoiding the nearest branches. Buildings loomed ahead of us, lights glittering against the growing darkness, and a deeper queasiness formed in my gut.

The demon would slow down soon—when it reached the city with all the possibilities for carnage that lay there.

I was speaking before I'd even thought the words through. "We have to—"

I cut myself off. Had to what? Stop and make some kind of last stand? I didn't for a second believe we could push back the demon right now, scattered and panicked and many of us wounded.

We'd always known the creature had more power than we could contend with directly. But all of our ideas to try to outsmart it had failed. Lady Northcott hadn't sounded as if she had much of a back-up plan when I'd talked to her an hour ago.

The enforcer in the front passenger seat twisted around to look at me. I expected annoyance, but all I saw in her face was desperation. She wanted me to have an answer.

I opened my mouth and closed it again. "I'm sorry."

Her lips pursed. "*You* shouldn't be apologizing. That thing is just... I wish we could feed the traitors who summoned that creature to it and watch it choke on them."

I doubted it would work exactly that way, but I couldn't deny the image was a little satisfying. Why weren't the Frankfords and my father and the rest of them out here facing the results of their crimes?

Because they'd have turned tail and run at the first glimpse of the destruction they'd brought down on us.

Seth's head tipped to the side. For an instant, I thought it was just with the motion of the car, but then his eyelids twitched.

"Seth!" I said with a twinge of hope. I stroked his forehead, soothing, mending, as well as I could. His body was still mottled with the marks of battle, but at least I'd stopped any bleeding. As for what was in his head...

His eyelids fluttered again and opened. He gazed up at me, his gray-green eyes hazy.

"Rose," he croaked, and my heart leapt.

"Right here with you," I said. "Do you remember what happened?"

He blinked slowly, his face going slack and then tensing again. "The demon. It was coming at all of you. It killed people. Did we—where are we?"

"In a minivan headed away from it as fast as we can

get," I said. There wasn't any point in worrying him with the question of what we'd do when we couldn't run anymore. "How do you feel? You blanked out for a while there. Does anything still hurt? I tried to help every way I could…"

He wet his lips and shifted his body a little as if testing it. "My head aches. Well, really, every part of me aches. But it's kind of a dull pain, not like I'm, I don't know, fatally wounded or anything."

A jolt of frustration shot through my relief. "You *could* have been. It could have killed you. What were you thinking, coming at it like that?" If it had been Damon, or Gabriel—Spark help me, I'd have expected that kind of brash charge from any of the other guys before Seth.

His brow furrowed. He gazed at the ceiling of the van distantly, lost in his thoughts for a several seconds.

"It was going to destroy the cars," he said. "And then it was going to destroy all of us. I couldn't think of anything else to do." His shoulders tensed as if he were about to try to sit up, but I clamped my hand down on his chest to hold him in place. "Did it work—did the other witches—"

"I think most of them got away," I said. The scene on the field had been too frenzied for me to keep track of much as we'd been peeling out of there ourselves. "You did distract it and keep it occupied for a few minutes longer than we'd have had otherwise. So I guess it was a good thing, even if it was also an incredibly reckless move and I hope I never have to see you do anything like that ever again."

Seth managed to chuckle, followed by a wince. "Sorry. If I could have done it without scaring you, I absolutely would have."

"I know." I leaned over him, pressing a kiss to his forehead. The van swayed as we took a corner too fast. We'd be back at the Assembly building soon—I'd have to leave him in the care of the medics. I couldn't play healer once there were real healers around and so many other people I had to try to save.

"Jin?" he said, that single syllable enough to convey an entire agonizing question.

"He has to be okay," I said. "I'd know if he wasn't."

"He was probably cheering me on," Seth said in a wry tone. "He said we needed to push outside our comfort zone. There was definitely nothing comfortable about jumping into that truck."

Jin had said that? When I wasn't around, I guessed. I might have asked more if Seth hadn't still looked so fragile despite his bulk—and then the van screeched to a halt. We'd reached the Assembly building.

Medics were already pouring into the underground parking garage with stretchers and salves to tend to the wounded we'd been able to collect. It occurred to me with a lurch of my gut that we'd probably left at least a few witches behind who'd been alive but too injured to run or even call for help. Maybe we couldn't have saved them anyway, but...

Oh, Spark help us all, how many had the demon already killed since then as it rampaged into the city?

Two of the women eased Seth away from me, offering reassuring murmurs. I let him go with a tearing sensation in my chest. An arm came around me, Jin's faintly smoky scent reaching me, and I couldn't contain a sob.

"He's awake?" Jin said, turning me and wrapping me in his embrace. "He's okay?"

"I think so," I said. I wanted to stay there enveloped in his warmth until the rest of the world was right again—but it might not ever be right again unless I helped. I squeezed my consort hard and forced myself to step back. "I'd better get upstairs and find out what the hell we're going to do now."

He followed me inside. The whole building was full of bedlam. The enforcers returning from our confrontation with the demon mixed with officials demanding answers and other panicked employees scurrying without much sense of direction. Voices echoed through the hall in a barely decipherable cacophony.

I couldn't see any of the officials I knew. I didn't see a single familiar face. Where was Naomi, or Thalia, or—

I spun around, jostled in the crowd, and found myself staring into a face that was both familiar and totally unexpected.

"Rose!" Imogen said, and threw her arms around me.

I hugged the younger witch back instinctively, my chin coming to rest on her mussed red curls. Imogen had come to my estate seeking shelter weeks ago—her aunt and uncle had been mixed up with the Frankfords and had tried to draw her into their clutches after she'd lost her parents and she and her younger sister had moved in with them.

It'd been a while since I'd seen her, though. After one of the Frankfords' surreptitious attacks—and my inability to fully explain what was going on—she'd packed up and headed back to her relatives. I'd known they'd been arrested along with the rest of the faction's witches, but I'd wondered how she was holding up.

"What are you doing here?" I said. She'd always been exuberant, but I hadn't expected quite this big a show of affection.

Imogen pulled back, her cheeks colored with an embarrassed flush. "Sorry. I just—I've felt so bad since I found out why you had to keep quiet and what you were really protecting me from. I heard something horrible was happening down here, and... I shouldn't have run away last time. I shouldn't have let myself get that scared. So I came. I don't know how much I can help, but I'll try, however I can."

I didn't know how much she'd be able to help either, unconsorted and without the use of her spark. But her words brought a bubbling of hope into my chest where I'd felt so vacant a moment ago.

There were so many of us, and we weren't giving up without a fight. The enforcer in the van had been right. There had to be some way we could overcome this thing.

And whatever that was, we had to figure it out as soon as we possibly could.

"Come on," I said, grasping her hand and catching Jin's eye so he'd follow us. "Let's find the witches in charge and see what we can still do. We're not beaten yet."

CHAPTER TWENTY-FIVE

Gabriel

The first sign we got that something was wrong was a curse ringing down the hall from one of the other offices. Kyler stiffened in his chair at the desk. Damon's head jerked up where he'd been sitting on the couch for the last half hour, glued to his phone with regular tapping of his thumbs. I wouldn't have been surprised if he were literally going through with his plan to try to find someone in the state who could deliver weapons of mass destruction on short notice.

"What was that?" Ky asked. I moved to the doorway. A voice talking, harsh and too low for me to make out the words, behind one of the other doors. A couple of officials ducked out of their offices and hustled down the hall away from us. My stomach sank.

"It's obviously not anything *good*," Damon said. His

tone was flippant but the shadows in his eyes told me he was just as worried as I was.

"I'll see what I can find out," I said.

Ky gave me a mock salute, his mouth pressed flat in an anxious line.

A small cluster of Assembly employees was forming at one end of the hall. One woman was jabbing her hand in the air frantically while another seemed to be trying to soothe the group with her soft words. A guy at the edge of the group shifted his weight from foot to foot, looking as if he'd rather be anywhere but there.

"What will we do?"

"They've called a meeting. They're working on a new plan right now."

"But if all the other plans didn't work..."

"Hey," I said in as friendly a voice as I could manage, giving the guy closest to me a gentle tap on the shoulder. "What's the news? How are our defenses against the demon?"

A couple of the witches shot me looks that were downright icy. The guy rubbed his mouth with a nervous twitch of his hand.

"There are no defenses," he said. "The demon went on the attack. Eight enforcer casualties reported so far, and twice that many who haven't been confirmed yet. They've pulled out."

"The demon's *here*," one of the women said, her voice squeaking on the last word. "It's already in the city."

Shit. My skin went cold. "What do they want us to do?"

"What are *you* going to be able to do anyway?" another official snapped.

The guy near me grimaced. "We don't know. No one's said anything definite. We're waiting to get word."

With their gazes turning increasingly hostile, I figured that was as good a time as any to extricate myself. I hurried back to our office to find Damon waiting in the doorway, his gaze even darker than before. He stalked inside when I reached him and swiveled on his heel to face me.

"Well? What did you get out of them?"

Ky was watching from the desk, his body still rigid. My body balked, and I suddenly understood the awkwardness of the people I'd just talked to on an even deeper level. It hadn't been only dismissiveness of some unsparked guy they didn't respect. Telling people horrible news felt horrible.

"Whatever they ended up trying to do to stop the demon before it got to the city, it didn't work," I said. "It broke through, killed a bunch of people, and as far as anyone knows, it's making its way into the city now."

It was Damon's turn to swear, much more creatively and emphatically than the voice we'd heard from down the hall. He paced back and forth on a five foot strip of the carpet, his hands clenching.

"What about Rose? Is Rose okay? Seth? Jin? They went out there too, messing some more with that stupid cage, didn't they?"

"It wasn't *stupid*," Ky broke in, but his face was even paler than usual, the flecks of his freckles standing out against his pallor. It was both his consort and his brother out there.

"They've got to be okay," I said quickly. "Alive, at least. The bond we formed with that second consorting —*we* wouldn't still be here if they weren't, right?"

My appeal to facts seemed to ground Kyler. He nodded, his chest rising and falling with a short breath. "Right. They're okay."

For now, none of us needed to add.

"Fuck," Damon muttered. "That thing is in the city—is it coming this way? Maybe it wants the assholes who messed with it and its kind for all those years."

"I don't know," I said. My stomach sank even lower, until I felt as if it were sitting on my feet. What the hell did I know about anything that was any use to us right now? Maybe the witches' dismissal hadn't been unprovoked. "This was the closest major city. It might have nothing to do with the witching community here."

Damon let out a sputter of a laugh. "Just wait. I'll bet a hundred dollars it's making a beeline for this fucking building right here. They wouldn't listen to us, they wouldn't listen to Rose, not when they should have, and now we're all screwed."

"They're already trying to figure out what to do next," I said, but that statement sounded weak to my own ears. I didn't have a huge amount of faith in the ruling body of Rose's witching Assembly either. "Rose must be on her way back with the enforcers and whoever else was out there. She saw firsthand what went down."

"No." Damon's tone turned abruptly flat. He strode

across the hall to the room we'd spent our first few nights in and started grabbing the scattered things we'd left there. I followed him, Ky coming up behind me.

"What are you doing?" I said.

He stuffed the clothes Rose had discarded earlier into a bag. "We should get over to the hotel suite, grab everything we want to keep from there, and get the car ready. Find that cousin of Rose's, maybe—she'll probably help. She's not an idiot."

"Get the car ready for *what*?" Ky said, crossing his arms. "We're not taking on that thing alone."

Damon's laugh was totally raw now. "Of course we're not. We're getting the hell out of town. There's putting up a good fight and there's knowing when you're beat. That monster has gotten enough chances at killing us—at killing Rose—already. It's in the city? Then we're getting out of here."

I stared at him. "You think Rose is going to agree to just abandon everyone here?"

"I think we can convince her. I think I'd be willing to haul her off under protest if that's what I have to do. What have these fuckers done this whole time except sneer at us and then use us whenever they have the opportunity? This is their problem. Let them fix it. We're nobodies' lackeys."

"But the whole city," Ky said quietly. "All the people here..." From his expression, I could tell he was doing the same calculations I was trying to. How many regular people who could never have imagined that anything like a demon existed had already been slaughtered by that fiend as it made its way into the city? How many more would die in just the next few hours?

"...are total strangers," Damon filled in for Ky. He glowered at us. "What about *our* people? Our families, back home? What if this thing doesn't stop here? We've got to get to them and be ready to take care of *them* if we have to. We look after our own. That's what matters."

"That's not how Rose is going to see it," I said.

Damon stepped right up to me, his eyes flashing. I'd thought, in those moments when we'd made Rose sigh and whimper between us just this afternoon, that we'd come to some kind of peace. It couldn't be more obvious from his expression now that his anger toward me hadn't gone anywhere.

"What the hell do you know about what's best for Rose?" he demanded. "Who made you grand lord over everything we do? At least I'm doing *something*. What's your great plan?"

I groped for an answer, feeling momentarily unbalanced. I'd come back to this sort of family, I'd promised I'd be here for these guys as much as for Rose, but how could I say that if I couldn't offer anything more right now than those nervous figures in the hall? *Let's just wait to get word.*

Fuck that. "I don't know yet, but I'm going to work something out," I said. "I'll find the Northcotts or whoever and figure out what we can do. But I know for sure that you're never going to convince Rose to leave here, and you're sure as hell not hauling her away unless you're thinking you'll chain her up like those assholes in the prison did."

Damon flinched. "She'll see," he said. "When we talk to her, when she realizes we're ready to go, she'll see." But he didn't sound so confident now.

He was scared. Maybe terrified. Why wouldn't he be? I raked my hand through my hair.

"Okay. Do whatever you've got to do. But—just stay close, all right? We don't know when Rose is going to make it back. We should be here when she does. I'll catch up with you as soon as I can, and I'll have better answers then."

I didn't wait to see if he'd agree. The appeal to being here for Rose should do the trick. I loped down the hall and up the stairs to the higher offices.

Lady and Mr. Northcott were both on their respective phones at opposite ends of their office, talking in strained voices. I didn't see any sign of the meeting the lesser officials seemed to have assumed was happening. I might have stayed put to wait for their attention, but the secretary hustled me out with a glare and a shove of magic when I hesitated.

"Leave them be," she said. "They're trying to save us all."

So am I, I thought, but I bit back the words.

Gwen Remington swept past me in the hall. "Lady Remington," I called after her, but before I could make any sort of appeal, she dismissed me with a jerk of her hand. The lock to her office thudded into place the second the door had closed behind her.

I hurried farther down, peering past doors left open into empty meeting rooms and offices. Up ahead, another door burst open with a squeal of its hinges, and Justin Brimsey stalked out.

"If it wasn't for that, we wouldn't be in this situation to begin with," he snapped at whoever he'd been arguing with. He shoved the door shut. His expression hardened when he saw me.

"I don't have time for this," he said, moving to march past me. His dislike for me—for all Rose's consorts, I was pretty sure—simmered closer to the surface than I'd ever seen it before.

Maybe that abhorrence should have made me falter. But at the same time I remembered who this guy was: the head of the Unsparked Relations division. The person who made the final call when it came to any clash between witching and unsparked interests.

A demon his community had unleashed was currently tearing apart one of the biggest cities on this side of the country. Maybe I couldn't blame him for being abrupt. But he might also be the person in the best position to get something done to save this city.

"Mr. Brimsey," I said, moving to intercept him. "We've got to get a plan together, fast. Someone has to step up and let everyone know how we're dealing with this."

He stopped, his glare nearly burning a hole in my forehead. "And do you think that person will be you?" he said with a disgusted curl of his lip. "Let us witching folk deal with our witching business."

My hackles rose, but at the same time a hot flush of shame washed over me. I *was* trying to take the lead, wasn't I? They were all scrambling to find a solution in their own way, these people who'd never have looked at me twice until I'd shown up at Rose's side. Why should they look to *me* for real guidance?

Or at least, for some kind of leader. There were other things I could offer, if I let myself.

Brimsey had started to brush past me. "Wait!" I said, grabbing his arm as carefully as I could. "Rose is witching folk. Rose can get things done."

His eyes narrowed. "Your consort seems to prefer to do whatever she pleases without much concern for what the rest of us think is the best course."

I didn't think that was a fair assessment, but this didn't feel like the right time to point that out.

"You have ideas the others aren't listening to?" I asked, tipping my head toward the room he'd come out of. "I want to hear them. I'll bring them to Rose. Work *with* us, and you can be calling the shots. Take the lead and we'll stand behind you. Just give us a chance. All we want is to see that demon gone and the city still standing."

Brimsey hesitated, still eyeing me. "Why should I think calling the shots with you is going to do me any good?"

I gave him a crooked smile. "We're running out of time and running out of options. You've got an idea we haven't tried yet? I can't promise Rose will listen to you, but she'll listen to me. And you know how much she's capable of."

He did. I could see him fighting with himself between the hope that I might be able to deliver what I was offering and his distrust of me and what my presence here at all meant to his ideas about witching kind. After a moment, his shoulders eased down.

"Come here," he said brusquely. "I'll show you what we need."

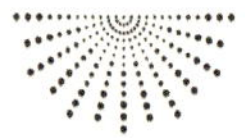

CHAPTER TWENTY-SIX

Rose

I hadn't found any of the major officials yet when Gabriel came upon me in one of the halls. His gaze took in the dirt and the smears of blood on my clothes in one swift sweep, and then he was tugging me to him, his arms tight around me, his head bent next to mine.

"Sprout," he said hoarsely, as if we were ten years old again, and by the Spark how much I wished we could go back to that time when the biggest problem we'd encountered was how to climb to the top of some tree Damon was set on scaling.

I hugged Gabriel back, giving myself permission to stop racing around and bury my face in the mossy-sweet scent of his shirt for a moment. I felt rather than saw his head rise again.

"Where's Seth?" he asked.

"Wounded but awake now," Jin said before I had to. "The witch medics are looking after him."

"The demon is already in the city," I said. "I can't— I need to find the Northcotts, or someone—we have to come up with some other way to push it back..."

Gabriel eased away from me and looked into my eyes, his own bright blue ones more serious than usual. "I might be able to help with that. But I don't think you're going to be happy about this strategy."

I knit my brow as I stared back at him. "Why? What do you mean?"

He glanced at the floor and back up again. "From the moment we heard your force had retreated, I've been trying to talk to the officials about next steps. I couldn't get anyone to speak with me except Brimsey—and I had to convince him that we'd follow his lead if we agreed with his route. He has an idea, one we could probably convince the rest of the Assembly of—if you support him and help make it work."

Justin Brimsey had agreed to ally himself with one of my unsparked consorts? I supposed that wasn't the strangest thing that had happened in the last week, or even the last twenty-four hours. "What is the idea? Why do you think I won't like it?"

Gabriel grimaced. "He thinks we need to involve the witches who are still recovering from the way the faction used them. I know you've wanted to protect them and keep them out of this conflict as much as possible... but he made a pretty compelling case. And nothing we've tried without them has worked so far."

My stomach twisted, but what he'd said was true,

and really, if we didn't step up then the recovering witches would be facing the demon in even more dire circumstances before the night was over.

I set my jaw. "Okay. I'll rally them as well as I can to tackle the demon with us. I don't know if that's going to be enough power even then, though. We need a strategy for how we use that power, or..."

I trailed off at Gabriel's expression. He looked as if the words he needed to say left a horrid aftertaste in his mouth.

"Brimsey has a strategy," he said. "And it's not for those witches to just fight alongside us. He thinks—and some of the accounts in the Frankfords' files do seem to support the idea—that the demon will be particularly interested in feeding off the energy of the witches it's familiar with. That the monsters have developed a 'taste' for those witches' specific magical 'flavor.' He wants to make a few adjustments to Seth's cage, and then we use them as bait. They draw it in and then slip away once it's trapped."

A jolt of revulsion rushed through me. It'd been bad enough thinking about asking Thalia and her charges to go up against the creatures that had tormented them. To encourage them to let the fiend feed off them again, to put them in an even more vulnerable position than they'd been before when at least the barriers on the portal had kept the demons distant...

But at the same time this plan made a sick kind of sense.

"What do the other officials think about the

situation?" I asked. "Has anyone come up with another option?"

"Not as far as I can tell," Gabriel said. "They all appear to be flailing with panic. Brimsey thinks our best chance of getting some kind of action pulled together is if you can convince the witches to participate and then join him presenting the proposal to the Northcotts and the others. As soon as possible."

Of course. I didn't need reminding of the urgency of the situation. I exhaled, a prickling ache filling my lungs.

I hadn't come up with any better plan on our drive here. Every moment we delayed, more people were dying out there. I didn't think we were going to get through the night without every one of us making sacrifices—even those who'd already given up too much.

"Okay," I said. "I'll go talk to them. Thank you for going to Brimsey—for working something out for when I got here."

"Is there anything else we can do right now?" Jin asked.

I hesitated. "Talk to the other guys. Tell them what's going on. Seth won't be on his feet for a little while, but it'll make more of a statement if I come to the meeting with as many of you as possible. And maybe Kyler can find some data to back the idea up even more. Jin, you could at least talk to Seth and see if he has any specific ideas for engineering the cage the way Brimsey is thinking. Someone's going to have to go out and gather the pieces..."

Logistics the Assembly would worry about once we settled on this course of action.

It would have been a comfort to bring one of my consorts down to the recovering witches' rooms with me, but there wasn't much they could contribute there. Those women trusted me. If I was going to make this ask, I had to be brave enough to face them on my own.

Gabriel squeezed my arm one last time, and he and Jin hurried off. I turned back to the stairwell, my heart heavy as I started to put together the pitch I'd need to make.

It'd only been maybe five hours since I'd gone down to the lower floor to help calm the witches who'd been so wrenched by the demons' approach. Some of them might not even be able to handle coming that close to it. But I guessed we didn't need all of them participating. As long as some were able to find the strength...

Thalia came out of the lounge room as I crossed the hall. Her face was drawn.

"It's bad, isn't it?" she said. "If you're back already, and—a few of the women aren't doing so well."

"It's bad," I confirmed around the lump in my throat. "I need to talk to all of you. Can you gather everyone— everyone who can manage it—into the lounge?"

She nodded, her mouth tightening more at my tone. As she hustled into the nearest dorm, I went into the lounge room and let myself sink into one of the armchairs. That was where my cousin found me a moment later.

"Rose!" Naomi said, clasping my shoulder, sounding both hopeful and frantic at the same time. "What's going on? Everyone came charging in—they haven't wanted to stop to tell me anything—"

I looked up at her. "I'll be explaining when everyone's here. I don't know what's going to happen tonight. I wouldn't blame you if you grab Aunt Ginny and Aunt Irene and get out of here."

Naomi gave a disbelieving laugh. "We wouldn't consider that for a second. We're here, and we're fighting this thing."

Those words managed to hearten me a little, but it was hard to hold on to that assurance as the recovering witches started to file in through the doorway. I stood up, taking a spot at the front of the room, unable to ignore the halting footsteps, the hunched shoulders. Half of the women here looked as if they'd just been through the same battle I had. I caught myself worrying my lip with my teeth and forced myself still.

Thalia came in with a dip of her head. This was all of them. A dozen witches the Frankfords' faction had manipulated and abused, some of them for decades.

My hands intertwined in front of me, clenching tight.

"This is going to be hard for me to tell you, and hard for you to hear," I said. "I'm so sorry about that. I wish we'd never ended up in this horrible position. The one thing I can offer to keep in mind while I explain is that there may be a way you can help, even if it is horrible. And whether you're able to do that is up to you. No one is going to force anything on you."

The witches stirred nervously in their seats. "Just tell us," Eloise said, her face pinched and pale.

I dragged in a breath. "Our most recent attempt to contain the demon failed. It's pushed into the city now.

We don't know what path it'll take or how far it'll go, but right now it's destroying everything around it, and the sooner we can act, the better."

A few of the witches turned completely white. Crystal dragged her legs onto the chair to hug her knees. A tremor ran through her skinny body. "I knew it," she mumbled. "I could feel it."

"What can we do?" Selena asked, her expression fierce. I wasn't sure she'd still look that confident when I told them.

"We're running out of plans," I said. "But there's one thing we haven't tried yet, that both the Assembly and I think could work. I never would have wanted to ask this of you... but we haven't been able to propel the demon into the trap we've made, so we're wondering if we could lure it. And the one thing we're sure it would be lured by is your magic."

Crystal flinched. Even Thalia stiffened. I swallowed thickly and barreled onward. "Like I said, no one would insist you help. We're just asking. Pleading. If you think you have the strength to stand up to this monster. This time it'd be your choice. You'd be doing it not to give someone else power but to be a part in cutting off this fiend's freedom. It'll be dangerous. I wouldn't pretend it won't be. But we'll do everything we can to make sure it's only a taste of your magic that you lose."

Someone drew in a ragged breath. Someone else started to cry, softly, with hitching breaths. My throat constricted even more. But Selena raised her ivory-coiffed head and said, "I'll do it. We'll take that Spark-forsaken creature down."

"I'll help," Thalia put in. "It's worth it. We have to stop that thing."

"What happens if we don't help?" Eloise said. "If it keeps coming—is it going to come *here*?"

"We don't know," I admitted. "We have no idea what it might do next. But it could make it this far." If the demon figured out that the witches it'd fed on before were right here for the taking, this might be exactly where it would want to go. But I couldn't bring myself to say that much.

The witches could put together the pieces on their own, no doubt. A few of them huddled together, talking in hasty tones. Crystal started to rock in her chair.

"It wants us," she murmured. "It wants us..." Her chin jerked up. "Let it try to have us, then. It's going to regret that it ever tried to devour us. We'll laugh when we see it captured."

The vehemence in her words seemed to spread through the gathering in an instant. Eloise straightened up, tucking her gnarled hands in her lap. "Yes," she said. "We can bring it to its knees." And around the room, other faces brightened in agreement.

I'd say my spirits lifted, but a sickening weight still pressed on my gut. This wasn't the sort of victory I'd wanted. If it would even be a victory in the end. But we had to try.

"I'll go to the Assembly and let them know you're ready to join the battle," I said. "Take the next little while to settle your thoughts and your nerves as well as you can. And if you change your minds—it's your decision, right through to the end."

I was just stepping into the hall when a wan man I'd seen at one of the last meetings ducked out of the stairwell. His expression when he caught sight of me was at least as distraught as it was relieved.

"Lady Hallowell," he said. "The authorities of the Assembly request your presence immediately. The demon... We don't know what to make of this at all."

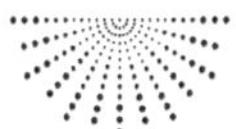

CHAPTER TWENTY-SEVEN

Rose

The key officials who'd been involved in addressing the demon problem were all gathered in one of the meeting rooms, bent toward a phone someone had set in the middle of the table. A voice crackled from the phone's speakers as the man who'd fetched me ushered me in.

"It's past the freeway now, moving southwest in a fairly straight line."

"Any further casualties?" Lady Northcott asked, her elbows rigid against the table top.

"No, it hasn't paid any attention to the cars or buildings it's gone past. It seems pretty intent on getting to wherever it's going. I'd estimate it's moving at up to twenty-five, maybe thirty miles an hour. That's the fastest we've ever seen it."

"And the captives?" Mr. Northcott said. "What's their status?"

The voice on the other end turned more raw. "Impossible to tell at this distance, especially with night coming in. It definitely isn't being careful with how it's holding them, but it seems to have suppressed some of its innate destructive energy. We're not seeing damage to the vegetation it's passing by. It may be tamping down on that energy to keep them alive for its purposes. I'll report more if we can make more out later."

"Please check in the moment anything changes," Lady Northcott said.

I came to a stop at the edge of the table as she reached to end the call. Had I heard all that right? My nerves shivered, uncertain of whether to be giddy or quaking.

"That's one of the enforcers who's monitoring the demon, isn't it?" I said. "It's heading back to the coast—to the Cliff?"

"It appears that way," Mr. Northcott said, sinking back in his chair. He didn't look happy about that fact. From the dire expressions around the table, I suspected my second assumption was right as well.

"It's grabbed some people too."

Lady Northcott nodded wearily. "After causing a great amount of wreckage and chaos in the west end of the city on the tails of your retreat, the creature caught up four—or maybe five, the reports aren't completely clear—bystanders and immediately set off in its current direction."

I supposed we could at least be relieved that the

fiend wasn't tearing apart the city anymore. But—why would it suddenly have retreated? And the people it had taken— "Do you think they're still alive?" I had to ask.

Remington grimaced at the other side of the table. "We haven't been able to determine that. What you heard from the report is as much as we know."

"Its course over the last ten minutes or so has been a direct line toward the Frankfords' property," Brimsey put in, his gaze on me evaluating. I wondered if he was aware that I'd already been trying to put the plan he'd pitched to Gabriel into motion. "We haven't seen activity anywhere near that purposeful from it before."

"We haven't," Lady Northcott agreed. "It does seem quite set on returning to that place as quickly as possible."

I couldn't for one second believe the demon had just wanted to take a little romp around our world and now it was going to head home quietly. "Has anything happened at the Cliff to bring it back?"

"Our people out there haven't observed any changes."

"Then—" My voice caught in my throat as an icy jolt of understanding hit me. It melted into a cold pool of horror in my stomach. "Oh, no."

"You have a take on what's happening?" Mr. Northcott asked. Everyone was studying me now. As if the demon taint to my spark gave me some kind of special understanding of what those monsters might want.

But I didn't need any special connection to them to put the pieces I had together.

"We figured the reason that one was able to break through the portal at all was the woman who died by the Cliff, don't we?" I said. "The blood spilled in violence—it helped the demon break through the barrier somehow. If it's bringing more people out there, avoiding destroying their bodies... I have to think it's planning on spilling all the blood it can so the rest of the fiends can come join it here."

Not just one but a whole horde of demons, all of them eager to treat our world like a carnival of brutality.

The officials around the table were silent for a moment. "That is our main fear as well," Lady Northcott said quietly. "To be honest, I was hoping you might have a different perspective that could also explain its actions."

I shook my head, my heart starting to race. "No. That has to be it. That's the only thing that makes sense. We have to get out to the Cliff first—stop it—we *wanted* it back near the portal. If we can prevent the blood-spilling and push the demon through, then we could seal the gateway up. All our problems solved."

Unfortunately, those felt like some tremendous "if"s right now.

"We can call on every witch in this part of the country," Remington said. "Bring all the power we possibly can to bear."

Brimsey looked to me again. "Have you had a chance to see if there are others who might be able to support our attempt after all?"

The recovering witches. I didn't know if we could still arrange any sort of a trap—we didn't *need* a trap if the thing was already out there by the portal—but their magic might still give us an advantage.

"I have," I said. "I spoke with Lady Ainsworth and the other witches from the faction a few minutes ago. They'll do whatever they can, including facing the demon, if it helps us push it out of this world."

"And what about you, Lady Hallowell?" Mr. Northcott said. "Are you well enough to go out there?"

I hadn't gotten to expend much magic against the demon this afternoon. I was tired just from the long day and the stresses that had come with it, but my spark flared when I focused on it. "I am, and of course I will."

Lady Northcott's mouth twisted. "From what we've seen, the way it responds to your magic compared to the rest of our people's... We may be counting on you by far the most." She turned to one of the lesser officials at the far end of the table. "See that a vehicle with plenty of space is arranged for Lady Hallowell and her consorts. We want her to rest and regain as much of her strength as possible on the journey to the coast."

The other woman bobbed her head and ducked out of the room. My gaze followed her. I hadn't expected special treatment. But then... maybe this *would* all come down to me. To me and the power I had, the power that flowed between my consorts and me.

"This won't be about sly plans or clever thinking," Lady Northcott went on. "It'll be brute force we need once we engage with the demon—to stop it long enough to free its captives, and then to force it back into its world. Can you coordinate that effort, Lady Hallowell?

Can I instruct our enforcers and the other witches to act as your support?"

My jaw went slack. I just stared at her and her husband for a moment. "I don't—I've got no combat training or anything like that. I think I know what to do, but—are you sure?"

The corner of her mouth twitched. "You've proven both resilient and resourceful more times than I can count in the last few months. If you're going to bring all your power to bear, you'll need as much support as you can get, I think."

Slowly, the others around the table inclined their heads, even Brimsey. My hands clenched at my sides. It all came down to me. Oh, by all that was lit and warm, by the five soul-bonds I carried, let me not fail.

"Find your consorts," Mr. Northcott said. "The car should be waiting for you in the garage by the time you get there. We'll be right at your heels."

Now I was staring at him. "You're coming too?"

"We're all coming," Remington said. "We're all that might stand between survival and the end of the world. I'm not sitting in my office when I could be bringing my magic to that fight."

A handful more witches in the mix—it might not make much difference. But it was something. More than I'd expected of them.

"I'll see you by the Cliff," I said. "I've got my phone. If anything important changes..."

"We'll let you know," Lady Northcott said.

* * *

The vehicle that the four guys and I found waiting for us in the underground parking lot looked like the same limo that had brought us to the Assembly in the first place. I almost laughed out loud.

"Not what you were expecting?" Damon said with an arch of his eyebrows.

"No," I said. "But it makes sense. They want me to try to rest on the way there." And possibly to bolster my store of magic in other ways, or they wouldn't have sent my consorts along with me. With the tension that was thrumming through my veins, I wasn't sure I'd be able to relax enough to sleep, let alone get up to anything more fun.

There was room for me to stretch out, at least, with only five of us instead of six. I felt Seth's absence as we climbed into the back like a missing limb. He'd been well enough to give me an impressive kiss when I'd slipped in to say good-bye, but the healer said he wasn't healed enough to go running around anywhere yet.

I was going to try not to think about the fact that the kiss we'd shared might be our last. That all of this might end in total catastrophe.

To at least make an attempt at that resting thing, I lay down on my seat with my head on Kyler's thigh. He brushed his fingers over my hair as I snuggled closer. Just that contact sent flickers of warmth through my chest to bolster my spark.

I was more powerful than I'd ever been before. I had the love of five amazing men supporting me. I *had* to be strong enough to defeat this demon. There just wasn't another option.

The engine rumbled as the driver on the other side of the privacy screen pulled out of the lot. Streetlamps and the light from restaurant windows flickered by in the deepening night. By the time we got out to the Cliff, it was going to be as pitch black outside as the demon's eyes. Could we hope that darkness would disorient the fiend a little bit too?

"What will you need from us once we're out there?" Jin asked.

"I don't know," I said. "I think it's going to come down mostly to me overpowering the demon, just for long enough to shove it back through that portal. We're going to have to be careful out there—if it kills anyone right on the Cliff, that could be enough to let the other demons through. So I guess... Stay back, have your batons ready if it comes near you—but mostly try not to let it get near you at all." Ruiz had brought us enforcer batons for each of the guys, but they hadn't been much use against the demon so far.

My consorts could take shelter among the enforcers and the other witches who'd be there—all of those who'd be lending me power, acting as a distraction while I figured out the best angle to hit the demon from... But we had to get its prisoners away from it first, alive or dead.

Spark help me, this wasn't going to be easy, I knew that much for sure.

"When you say it all comes down to *you*," Gabriel said slowly.

"My magic, with the demonic influence in it, is the

only energy that's had much effect on the thing," I said. "So that's the plan. Focus everything on me. If I can get it close enough to the Cliff... I'm sure I've got enough power in me to force it into the cave from there. I'll just need the right moment, maybe for the other witches to distract it so it's not bracing itself against me..."

"They're asking a lot," Damon muttered.

"No," I said. "They're asking exactly as much as they should. They're all going out to face it too, you know—the Northcotts and the other officials. They can't help that what my father did to me gives me an edge no one else can replicate. Every witch in the city right now will be joining the fight however they can, even Thalia and her group."

Dad had talked about the power he'd ensured for me as if it'd been a gift he'd given. Maybe in some ways it was, even if it wasn't one I'd ever have wanted, even if he hadn't really meant it for that purpose when he'd poured that magic into my mother's womb.

I closed my eyes, trying to let the hum of the limo's engine lull me. We'd reach the Cliff in just a couple hours, ahead of the demon unless it managed to start outpacing cars. And then I'd find out just how much power I had in me—and whether it was enough to save us all.

CHAPTER TWENTY-EIGHT

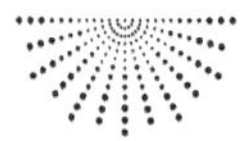

Damon

The damp salty wind felt even thicker than the last time we'd been out at the Cliff, or maybe it just seemed that way in the dark. The globes of enchanted light the witches had set up across the grassy yard of the Frankfords' seaside property only penetrated the night thinly. They made everyone look like specters, sallow and blurred along the edges.

Of course, the demon was going to provide its own light when it got close enough. We could already make out the faint reddish glow in the distance, far enough away that I couldn't see it moving when I stared at it. But every few minutes when I glanced over, it loomed a little larger.

Most of us weren't set up in the yard anyway. We'd gathered on the fallow fields on the other side of the country road about a hundred feet from the laneway, where the witches were hoping we'd intercept the monster before it made it to the Cliff and carried out its murderous intentions. I didn't think any of them had a clue how close blood needed to be spilled before it might help the other demons escape. We were all hedging our bets here.

At least mine were riding on Rose. If she couldn't get us through this, it'd all be a lost cause anyway.

"Is there any new information from the enforcers tracking the demon?" Rose asked one of the enforcers, who seemed to be some sort of commanding officer. The other woman shook her head, and Rose bit her lip.

"They probably can't see much more than we can," I said. "It's not as if they'll want to cozy right up to it."

"Do you think there's any chance it'll have left the people it grabbed alive?" Kyler asked, his forehead creased with worry.

"There's no way to know," Rose said. "The demons might need an actual killing right at the Cliff for the effect to work. We might still be able to save them."

A prickle of uneasiness ran over my skin. I could almost make out the demon's form now: the curve of its knobby head, the hunch of its shoulders. My mouth went dry. I forced myself to swallow.

I'd faced it before and come out no worse for wear. I wasn't letting some monster cow me. Not while Rose needed us here.

She was gazing toward that glowing shape too, her expression torn. Before she could leave us there with the witches we barely knew, which she'd have to before much longer, I grabbed her hand and pulled her to me.

There was nothing easier or more natural than burying my fingers in her hair and claiming her mouth with mine.

For luck. For whatever power might flow from me to her. For everything I had to give.

She was gripping my shirt when I eased back. I leaned my forehead against hers.

"I love you," I said. My voice came out hoarser than I really liked.

Her lips formed a bittersweet smile. "I love you too." She turned to the others, leaning in to kiss Gabriel, and then Jin, and then Ky. "I love all of you. And I'm looking forward to spending the rest of our long lives together."

She couldn't sound completely confident, but the words gave me a rush of satisfaction anyway. She wasn't sure we'd make it through the night. The rest, I knew, she couldn't have meant more.

Our consort stepped away from us to head down the lane, to wait at the front of the ambush. The enforcers around me and the other guys nudged us back, farther into the field where the other less trained witches who'd joined the fight were clustered.

I submitted to the prodding only because I knew Rose would falter if she looked down the road and saw us still there within easy reach of the demon. My hand tightened around the magical baton the enforcers had lent me. It might not be good for much against a supernatural creature from another dimension, but if I could make it hurt, I would.

Another surge of that discomforting sensation washed over me. Somewhere behind us, one of the witches—probably one of the ones who'd fed that thing before—let out a soft whine, and someone else started to murmur to her in soothing tones. I glanced at the other guys and saw their expressions tense in the dim light too. The amount of power that thing had...

No, I wasn't going to think about that. I wasn't going to think about anything except Rose's strength. It might be a demon, but tonight it was going up against an angel in her full glory.

The earth trembled beneath our feet. The thing was lumbering on at quite a clip according to the reports we'd gotten. Enough to make it feel like the approach of an earthquake.

"You know," Ky murmured, "this is probably a totally corny thing to say, but I'm going to say it anyway, because, well, killer demon heading our way, you know."

"Just spit it out, Brainiac," I said.

His lips twitched into a smile. "I'm glad we came together again. I'm glad we had at least a few months like this, even if a lot of that time we couldn't focus on a whole lot other than not getting caught or killed. It's been... It's been good."

"Yeah," Gabriel said softly. "It has been. I'm sorry I wasn't around for all of it."

"To making it through to the next great adventure," Jin said wryly, raising his hand as if making a toast.

I'd spent a lot of the last few months feeling as if I was still only on the fringes of the group, only included in it because of history and Rose's affection. But right then, in the hazy magical light streaking through the depths of the night, I had to say it really had been good.

Maybe we didn't fit together quite as easily as we had back when we were kids, but we did fit, even me.

There wasn't anywhere else I'd rather have been right now, and not just for Rose.

"To the next great adventure," I said, echoing Jin's tone. We knocked knuckles the way we would have clinked glasses.

The ground shook again, harder this time. The eerie sensation in the air just hung there now, wafting stronger and then ebbing but never completely fading. The hairs all up my arms rose. I braced myself, my gaze fixed on the glowing form rambling toward us. It was almost here.

The magical lights caught the creature's twisted face —and the bodies dangling where it was clutching them under its left arm. They rocked with its movements, limbs limp, but I thought I saw one pale hand jerk as if trying to pull free.

Damn. They really might have survived that horrific trip.

Rose must have given some gesture, because the witches at that end of the field sprang into action. The air warbled with a different sort of energy, one that jolted me in a way I didn't mind.

The demon halted, its head swinging as it sought out its attackers. Its eyes were so dark they seemed to blend into the night around it, as if it had two holes leading right through its smoldering face out the back of its skull.

Sparks of magic burst across its side. My hand found the sapling next to me and gripped it hard. I couldn't tear my gaze away.

The magical assault didn't seem to have hurt the

demon any, but I guessed that wasn't the point. As more flashes and flares flickered around it, Rose appeared on the road where it must have meant to cross, her body whirling, her hair streaking out around her like a spray of shadow.

The demon gave a deep snarl. Rose thrust out her hands, and the creature's left arm spasmed, shooting out to the side as if she'd shoved it.

The bodies of its victims tumbled to the ground. With a hiss of magic like a rising wind, a ripple of movement spread through the enforcers along the road. The demon lunged after its prey, but Rose spun again, and the other witches drew in their magic. The demon stumbled backward a couple paces. A magical wind wrapped around the slumped forms and yanked them away from the fiend into the midst of the gathered witches farther afield.

"Medic!" someone called. The figures rushed through the darkness, reassembling for the next part of the plan. Retreating as far as they dared now that they had the captured people safely away. Gabriel motioned to us, and we all edged back several more feet from where Rose stood, like she'd instructed.

My heart thumped fast in my chest as I watched her pale figure on the road, so slight compared to that hulking monster. This was the hard part. She had to force that thing across the long yard of the Frankfords' property and into that cave, and the other witches might not be able to help her much at all.

She'd said she was going to ask the other witches to distract it, and they were definitely holding up that end of the deal. Light quavered across the demon's back and haunches, making it lurch and gnash its teeth. As it swiped toward the edge of the road where the witches were well out of reach, Rose threw a burst of magic at it. The wind whistled, and the creature tumbled across the road and into the yard, heading toward the Frankfords' house there.

But only part of the way. It leapt up with another of those guttural snarls and sprang back at Rose. With a slash of her arms, she managed to deflect it and shove it back, but it landed a little closer to her and the enforcers again. She heaved, and it skidded another few paces toward the Cliff. It roared and flung its massive body toward her with a crackling of its unearthly energy that rattled the roots of my teeth.

They pushed back and forth like that a few more times, the demon gaining a little ground back and losing it and gaining it again. Even in the dim light, a sheen of sweat glinted on Rose's face. Her chest heaved with panted breaths. My own lungs constricted.

It was wearing her down. The witches were still tossing their own flashes of magic at the creature, but its attention was solely focused on Rose now, and she couldn't force it across all that terrain while it was fighting her every step of the way.

The demon tried to dodge to the side, around Rose, and she hurled it back again—but its claws dug into the packed dirt of the road, holding it from sliding farther. Its opaque gaze swiveled toward the witches beyond her.

It'd go to the Cliff, all right, but only if it had bodies it could break over the rocks there, blood it could spill for its own power. Rose was strong... but that thing might be stronger.

My hands itched for something—a pistol, a bazooka, a missile launcher, I'd take whatever—even though I knew with dread curled around my stomach that I couldn't have helped her no matter what weaponry I had in my hands. Bullets and bombs would bounce right off it.

So that was it? All we could do was stand here and watch as the last hope this world had fell apart? Wait for that thing to spray all our blood across the Cliff?

At the final thought, I found myself glancing down at my hand. At the starburst of a scar where I'd mingled my blood with Rose's, offering my soul in return for hers. A chill flooded me.

She needed distractions. She needed that monster by the Cliff. And it wanted a victim to slaughter.

I couldn't fight it like a lion. Did I have it in me to be the lamb?

Nausea pooled in my gut, but at the same time my jaw clenched with cold resolve. Someone had to do something, or we were going to lose everything. And I trusted Rose. I'd trusted her with my heart, with my life, with my soul. Compared to everything we'd already been through, offering myself up like this was barely anything at all. I knew she'd get me through it.

Gabriel must have caught a hint of my intention in my face. "Damon," he started, frowning.

I met his eyes, and a wild grin twisted my mouth. With a jerk of my hand, I snapped a branch off the sapling. "I'll be right back," I said, and bolted for the road.

Someone else called my name, but my pounding feet didn't falter. I tore across the road and onto the grass of the yard, pushing myself faster with every stride.

When I passed the house, I figured I had enough of a head start to make it to my goal. I let out a whoop in case the demon hadn't noticed me yet and scraped the broken end of the narrow branch across my palm.

Blood welled up along the stinging line. I kept running, tossing the stick aside, holding my hand to the air in the hopes the breeze would carry the scent the creature was craving to it.

My stomach had balled into a knot, but I focused my mind down to two thoughts. The witches had used their blood to hold the demons at bay—the blood I gave freely couldn't help it. And Rose would come for me, for it, before it had a chance to use a single drop in my body for its own ends.

Another roar sounded behind me, but this one sounded almost eager. So eager my bones shivered at the sound. I threw myself forward even faster, past the scattered line of trees, out to the rocky ground at the edge of the Cliff.

The salty wind smacked my face. I dropped down by the start of the path leading down that stone face, letting myself slump on the ground, pathetic and vulnerable. And with a lurch of the ground, the demon came charging to take me.

CHAPTER TWENTY-NINE

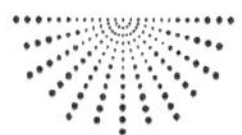

Rose

I heard the shouts and caught a blur of motion down the road from the corner of my eye, but I *felt* Damon's mad dash toward the Cliff down to the pit of my spark. One of my consorts was flinging himself into danger. Laying his life on the line.

The awareness ripped through me—and the demon's head turned. For the last several minutes, it had been completely focused on getting past me to the witches I was blocking it from snatching up, but Damon had caught its attention. Its opaque eyes narrowed and its crooked nostrils flared. My gut lurched, but at the same time I understood.

This was what Damon had wanted. He was playing bait like we'd meant to have the faction's witches do. Only there wasn't any trap here, just the Cliff—the Cliff where the fate of the entire world might rest on my reaching him in time.

The demon pushed away from the road with a roar, hurtling in the direction I'd spent the last several minutes trying to shove it. I couldn't be completely happy about that now. I threw myself after the fiend.

My feet smacked the matted grass of the yard, my breath raw in my throat. My limbs were already aching from all the magicking I'd thrown at it so far. But I had to dredge up more. Somewhere inside me, I had to find the power to see this last gambit through.

With a flick of my hands, I sent energy to my feet to speed each step along. The demon barreled between two of the trees near the edge of the Cliff, smashing them onto their sides with a shower of bark shards. I raced after it, pulling more and more light and warmth from my spark to the edges of my body. I might only get one chance to do this right.

Damon was sprawled on the rocks right by the cliffside. The glowing balls of magic my fellow witches had left floating through the air turned his skin a sickly yellow. A dark streak of blood colored his palm. His shoulders were tensed, his eyes wide and jaw clenched.

His terror as the demon careened toward him rang through me, bringing tears to my eyes. I blinked them away and sucked in a breath. Leaping past the splintered tree trunks, I planted my feet on the rocky ground already half a step into my magicking.

The demon pounced. I sent all the force I could summon, all my need to protect my consort, ramming into the monster's back. Its clawed hands were already snatching at Damon's body—

My magic hit the fiend and propelled it farther, faster, over the edge of the cliff. In a second, it had tumbled right over.

It shrieked as it fell, claws scrabbling against the rock with a horrible screech. Damon rolled away from the edge, clutching his arm to his chest.

"Go get it!" he shouted. "I'm fine. Go!"

My pulse hiccupped anyway, but I couldn't stop to check on him, or we might both be dead in another instant. My feet flew over the pebble-strewn ground to the path cut into the sheer rock.

The demon had caught hold of that ledge farther down, about halfway between me and the cave. It clambered toward me with a low reverberating growl, its glow flickering around it like flames in a breeze. Damon had gotten it so close to the cave, to the portal I needed to shove it through. I just had to push it the rest of the way.

The path didn't give me much room to move through a form. I focused on my arms, whipping the energy within me around me and out, stepping backward and forward in time.

The surge of magic I cast out propelled the demon a few feet farther down the Cliff, but that was all. Every muscle in my body throbbed.

I couldn't let this become another standstill. I had to end this battle *now*.

The rough rock my hand had come to rest against bit into my fingers. My thoughts darted to the recovering witches, to their stories of blood and skin offered up to hold the demons back. A sacrifice offered up for that purpose—a power greater than anything the demons could produce in response.

Did I have enough blood in my whole body to contain this creature now that it was free in our world—to contain it and still be conscious enough to hold that spell?

My instincts said no. But as I dug down deep to draw all the power I could from my spark, the tearing ache of that magicking made my breath catch with a sudden idea.

The possibility that had just crossed my mind brought a fresh ache with it, sharper and more poignant. That emotion only convinced me I was right. A sacrifice wasn't a sacrifice unless you let go of something you cared about.

To destroy this menace, I would give up the thing I'd cared about most after my consorts. And I'd pray that my sacrifice would see my purpose through.

The demon heaved itself toward me again. I raised my hands and spun around on that narrow outcropping of rock, trusting my feet to find purchase, trusting my balance to hold. Trusting in the great Spark that blessed witches like me with its power.

"All that is lit and warm in the world, hear me now," I called out. "Let me bleed my spark, let me put all of it into this magicking. I give every piece of it I need to drive this demon back to whence it came."

My spark flared in my chest and seemed to split. Agony stabbed through me as a fragment of that flame snapped from the light in my chest and flowed to my hands. Gritting my teeth against the pain, I whirled my arms in another magicking shaped around that piece of my spark.

My nerves wrenched even more as the light left me—but it burst into a blazing glow that walloped the demon and sent it skidding down the path, all the way to the cave's entrance. I scrambled after it on wobbly legs, with ragged breaths, already reaching inside myself to tear away another piece of the source of magic I'd been born with.

This was more than blood, more than skin, more than bone could have been. It was the core of who I was, who I'd been. But not who I'd be, not anymore—if I survived this battle at all.

The demon tried to rear up, but I was ready for it. With a thrust of my hands that seemed to rip me open from the inside out, I tossed it sideways into the cave. The ache crept right up to the back of my skull. My muscles were burning.

I couldn't stop. I had more. I could give everything, if that was what it took.

The demon staggered upright on the floor of the cave. Its eyes were as flatly black as always, but they looked wider now, its challenging grimace less certain. It hadn't expected this. It hadn't expected me.

Behind it, the starker glow of the portal whirled. One demonic face and then another swam in its depths. Clawed hands scrabbled at the edges. The power in the seal wavered, and my stomach flipped over.

Even without blood spilled, we'd almost been too late.

My knees started to give. *No.* I drew a form with my limbs as I sank down to the cave floor, pulling more and more of my spark from its place nestled deep inside me. With every stream of that purest magic I tore away, another knife of agony sliced through me. My vision was blurring.

I balled the blaze in my hands and whipped it at the demon with all my strength. The force drove it backwards, crashing into the portal and through. A clatter of rasping voices in a language I didn't understand carried out. Something screamed. The cave shuddered.

I pushed harder, condensing all the magic I'd gathered into a searing light and smashing it against the portal, jerking my arms and flicking my wrists to bind, to seal, to implode.

Strands of the portal's red glow broke off and flowed through the magic pressing inward on that opening. They spiraled into the vacant space within, chunks of rock falling after them. Cracks raced across the cave ceiling.

There was nothing left of me but the pain pounding through my veins and the pulsing circle of the portal contracting and contracting with each swivel of my wrists.

A mass of rock tumbled from the ceiling. A smaller piece clipped my shoulder. My whole body was already throbbing so much I barely registered the blow.

A demon eye pressed against the shrinking portal; a demon claw jabbed through. I couldn't back away yet. I had to see this done, all the way, until I knew the greatest mistake witching kind had ever made was finished.

Numbness spread over my skin and into my flesh. I couldn't feel my hands anymore, even as I wheeled my arms to twist the magic clogging the portal even tighter.

A groan so unearthly it turned my gut to water pierced the air. Then the portal closed completely with a crackle and a smell like hot tar.

The cave crumbled inward at the same moment, rocks showering down over the scorched wall where the portal had vanished. My head spinning, I scrambled backward.

The falling stones battered my legs as I dragged myself through the cave mouth. The sea hissed and foamed below and the wind warbled above, and the darkness closed around me. I groped for the path and nearly tumbled right over the edge of that rocky outcropping to meet the waves below.

Footsteps thumped against the stone. Arms wrapped around me, hefting me up. "We've got you," a voice said. "We've got you. You'll be okay." And someone else made a sound like a swallowed sob.

It is *okay*, I wanted to tell her, if I could have found my mouth, my vocal chords, amid the pain raging through me. *They're gone. They're done. They can't hurt anyone here ever again.*

I drew in a breath with an even deeper flare of agony, and I wasn't aware of much of anything for a long time after that.

CHAPTER THIRTY

Rose

I got the impression it pained Brimsey a little, standing up in the row of officials paying tribute during this ceremony. The Northcotts and Remington and most of the others at least looked honestly happy, but even after everything, the head of Unsparked Relations couldn't keep that slight curl of distaste from his mouth.

Well, let him find us distasteful. I was standing with my consorts, alive and on legs that would hold me, in front of nearly everyone who was everyone in the witching world, and they were here to recognize us.

The late summer day was crisp and clear, the breeze over the patio on the Assembly building's rooftop carrying a hint of the coming fall. The officials who'd been most involved in the defense against the demon were arranged in a row behind the stately podium. The other guests were scattered among the small potted hedges.

Lady Northcott was at the podium now, speaking in a voice as crisp and clear as the air, but warmer.

"And it is thanks to all that we are all here to help this city rebuild and to regain the footing of our witching community. We must recognize the risks taken and sacrifices made by Lady Hallowell and her five consorts. As such, on behalf of the Assembly, we hereby certify that this consorting, while unusual, is completely valid in every way, and Lady Hallowell's consorts must be treated as full members of the witching community. We will be opening inquiry into the historical basis for similar consortings so that all witches may have as much freedom as they deserve. And tonight we will dine in honor of our bravest peers."

She dipped her head to us, and my throat tightened with joyful emotion. Gabriel squeezed my left hand, Kyler tucking his fingers more closely between mine at my other side. Damon raised his chin with a defiant flash of his eyes as if he thought he still needed to prove something here. Jin beamed at me, and Seth let out a long exhale, as if he'd only just realized it really was all over.

We were safe. We were free.

The people who were gathered around us launched into applause. The Northcotts motioned us up to the small table set next to the podium, where they had an official consorting record ready for us to sign.

We shook everyone's hands, and then the gathering dispersed to reassemble downstairs in the dining hall. Naomi and then my aunt Ginny grabbed me in a hug,

Aunt Irene watching with a hesitant smile. The recovering witches, all of them bright-eyed and steady despite their encounter with the demon just a few days ago, came over with brief touches and words of gratitude. Knowing the demons had no more access to this world had done more for their healing than any spell could have.

We waited until they'd all headed down the stairs before we moved to follow. Gabriel slipped his arms around my waist, holding me for just a second before we went into the stairwell.

"What do you think?" he said, softly but lightly. "Was it worth all the trouble?"

I didn't think he meant just the outside struggles we'd been through. His embrace brought a quiver into my chest: the flicker of all that remained of my spark. Overcoming the demon and sealing the portal hadn't taken all of my magic, but it had taken a lot. No one was ever going to look on in awe while I cast a spell again.

But I'd found that realization less painful than I might have expected. If we were safe, I didn't need to be doing spectacular magic. Enough to heat up a cup of tea or soothe a small burn if that tea spilled should be plenty for the peaceful life I'd like to lead.

If I felt a slight ache, it disappeared as soon as I thought of the consequences we'd have faced if I hadn't managed to rip myself apart like that. There was nothing in the last few months that I could honestly say I'd change. In every case, the alternative might have been so much worse.

"Absolutely worth it," I said, hugging Gabriel's arm against me. "I wouldn't change a moment of it."

* * *

One week later

It'd been a long time since Hallowell manor had seen this much activity. My mother's entire extended family—consorts and cousins and all—had flown in to join our homecoming celebration. Lesley and Imogen had come by, and my consorts had invited their parents. Everyone was grabbing food off the platters on the dining table and sipping wine and gabbing away in what sounded like upbeat tones. Our return to the estate appeared to be getting off on the right foot.

We hadn't been gone that long, but it felt like a larger homecoming than it was in literal terms. This was the first time my guys had been able to acknowledge that my house was going to be their home too. I might have to hide my magic, but my consorts and I weren't going to hide our relationship anymore.

Meredith came up beside me, holding a tray with a couple of the cleared platters. I'd tracked down the estate's former manager, the woman who'd been the closest thing I had to a mother most of my life, as soon as we'd gotten back, and asked her if she'd consider letting me rehire her. My stepmother had booted her out coldly and abruptly a couple months ago, before the estate was mine, before I'd been sure I'd get to keep it once it was.

To my relief, Meredith had agreed without hesitation.

"It's a fine family you're building for yourself," she said now, a quiet smile playing with her lips. "You're doing me proud. And I can't fault your taste in young men."

I laughed. "Only maybe my inability to choose between them?"

"Ah, why should you choose if they all enjoy being by your side?" She winked at me and ambled on to the kitchen, where she'd been helping the staff.

I wasn't sure everyone shared that sentiment. Aunt Irene still looked a little awkward as she glanced from Gabriel chatting with Naomi to Jin making Seth and Kyler's mother, Mrs. Lennox, exclaim over his latest painting, which was hung in the living room.

Weirdly, even though it was Mrs. Lennox who'd gotten the most agitated by the Frankfords' spell that had stirred up paranoia in all of the guys' parents about their association with me, she seemed to be taking our joint relationship a lot more in stride than Mr. Lennox was. He'd been standing in the corner nursing a beer for most of the hour since they'd arrived, brushing off my attempts to make small talk. He didn't seem angry or anything, just uncertain.

"He'll come around," Seth said, tucking his head beside mine from behind. I guessed he'd seen where my gaze had traveled to. "It's not a standard relationship in the regular world either. It'll just take some time for him to get used to the idea."

"Do you think Damon's mom will too?" I couldn't help asking. She'd begged off attending the party altogether at the last minute, and Damon's expression when he'd told me had made it clear he suspected she was just making excuses, even if he hadn't admitted that.

"I guess we'll see. Damon's happy. We're all happy. That should count for more than anything else."

"Yeah." I rested my hand over Seth's where it had settled on my waist. "I guess we're always going to get some weird reactions, even if we're not overt about what's going on between us. One woman going around with five guys..."

Seth shrugged. "Let them be weird. What they think has nothing to do with who we are or what we stand for." He pecked me on the cheek. "You know you're not supposed to be worrying on our behalf. We get to decide how much awkwardness we can handle."

He was right. I wasn't concerned so much about how anyone saw me but about how the guys' friends and neighbors would react as well as their families. But that really was their decision to make. I let out my breath and went to ask Jin's mother about her latest additions to her beloved garden.

Damon wandered by us with a wary but respectful bob of his head to Mrs. Lyang and a smile for me. When he stopped by the table, his fingers worried at the bandage on his left forearm while he considered what he'd eat next.

I sidled over to him after I'd finished catching up with Jin's mom. "Is your arm bothering you?"

"What? No. It's fine. You know, the same."

I didn't totally trust Damon to tell me that he was in excruciating pain if he thought avoiding mentioning it would save me a little distress. I raised my eyebrows at him, and he fixed me with a determined stare.

"Really," he said. "I promise, I'd tell you if something was up. I don't want this thing messing me up any more than you do."

The demon had managed to get one of its claws into his arm before I'd tossed it over the Cliff. The Assembly's medics had sealed the wound easily, but a silvery gray mark like a splintered bullseye remained that their efforts hadn't been able to remove. Damon had decided he'd rather cover it up than show it off at this gathering. And to remind himself not to scratch at it, he'd said.

It hadn't shown any signs of being anything other than a strange scar, even ten days later. Seth's wounds from the demon's earlier attack had faded away faster, but it hadn't physically touched him. Maybe, just maybe, I should accept that the mark might not hurt Damon any more than my diminished spark still hurt me.

"Okay," I said, and bobbed up on my toes to kiss him. He made a pleased sound that spoke of all the things he'd have liked to do if we hadn't been surrounded by company.

Later that night, after the guys' parents had headed back into town and my guests had retired to their rooms, I climbed into bed with my five consorts, fitting snuggly between them all.

"First order of business now that we're getting settled back in," I said, resting my head on Ky's shoulder. "Bigger bed for the master bedroom. We should all have room to stretch out."

"I don't know," Damon said, hugging me to him. "I'm just fine like this."

I stuck my tongue out at him, and he grinned. "I'm not saying I *want* more space right now," I said. "I'd just like to give you all the option. Maybe a couple of day beds in case someone wants one to themselves some nights?"

"Bed shopping added to tomorrow's agenda," Gabriel said teasingly.

"What else is on the agenda?" Jin asked in an unusually thoughtful tone. "What does the lady of Hallowell manor *do* when she's not unraveling conspiracies and fending off unexpected enemies?"

"I'm not sure," I said. "I mean, I'll find some ways to occupy myself. I was going to put together that modern witching history... Maybe I can help the Assembly's investigations into the history of nontraditional consortings. And I was thinking..."

"What?" Seth prompted gently when I hesitated. He rubbed my foot where he was sprawled at the end of the bed.

"Maybe I'm not the best person to do this. I mean, I don't have any formal training in social services or whatever. But I thought it might be useful if I could spearhead some sort of program to help witches who are having trouble finding a suitable partner in the witching community. Come up with strategies to allow them to connect with unsparked men who might be a good fit."

"I think your experience has been more than good enough training for that," Gabriel said. "And I think you can find a way to accomplish just about anything you want to, Sprout."

I snuggled deeper into my consorts' combined embrace. It had always felt amazing, being with these guys, but now, without any threats hanging over us, even my fractured spark danced with a brilliant warmth. We'd fought, and we'd won. The long life together I'd dreamed about could really be ours, from this night onward.

"Is there a relationship agenda too?" Ky asked, rumpling my hair. "Do you want us all moving onto the estate permanently?"

"Of course," I said. "I mean, if you want to. I'm not going to be offended if you'd rather spend some of your time in town or wherever. I just... I'd love to have you here as much as you want to be here. I know you have the rest of your lives too."

Ky chuckled. "I have a few clients who are going to be overjoyed that I can remind them to reboot their computers again. I don't think that requires I keep my apartment, though. It's not exactly far from here to town."

"I have no desire to spend any more time in that shitty basement my idiot landlord passed off as an apartment," Damon muttered. "Especially not when I could be here with you instead."

"You know I'm already moved in," Gabriel said.

"And me," Jin said. "I'll probably be doing some

traveling to gather new pieces for display once the gallery is rebuilt, but there's nowhere I'd rather come back to than this house."

"Maybe you're going to need me to build an addition to go with that bigger bed," Seth joked. I poked him with my toes. He caught them, running his thumb over the arch of my foot. Then his hand went still. "I guess there are other things we'll need to talk about at some point. Like... kids?"

"Kids?" I repeated, with a shiver of emotion that was nervous and joyful all at once. I hadn't let myself think about anything that far in the future when we still hadn't been sure we'd get to have any future at all.

"Your Assembly has to approve, right?" Gabriel said. "Now that they've made us official and everything... Not that I'm saying I think we should get started on that step *just* yet."

"But sometime," I said, the shiver turning into a full-out flutter in my chest.

"Sometime," he agreed.

"Just saying this now," Damon said, with a kiss to the side of my neck. "We all know Rose and I will make the cutest kid. So clearly I should go first."

A laugh sputtered out of me. "You figure we're going to have a rotation, then? Not just leave it to chance?"

"Hey, if you want the best..."

"Hold on a second," Ky said. "I don't think we *do* all 'know' that. Should we bring an objective third party in to evaluate our respective cuteness factor?"

Jin snickered. "Knowing you, you've probably already got an expert in mind."

At that remark, we all cracked up. I lay back, soaking in the warmth and love of the five men who'd joined their lives to mine.

What we had here, what we'd made together, it was right. It was good. And I couldn't imagine ever feeling lost or lonely again, not while I had my consorts by my side.

ABOUT THE AUTHOR

Eva Chase lives in Canada with her family. She loves stories both swoony and supernatural, and strong women and the men who appreciate them. Along with the Witch's Consorts series, she is the author of Their Dark Valkyrie series, the Dragon Shifter's Mates series, Demons of Fame Romance series, the Legends Reborn trilogy, and the Alpha Project Psychic Romance series.

Connect with Eva online:
www.evachase.com
eva@evachase.com

www.ingramcontent.com/pod-product-compliance
Lightning Source LLC
Chambersburg PA
CBHW021306190726
48288CB00003B/721